G000066574

THE LOST ORPHAN OF CHEAPSIDE

VICTORIAN ROMANCE

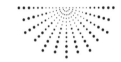

DOLLY PRICE

CONTENTS

1. Early Days — 1
2. Visitors — 6
3. Uncle Davey — 11
4. Mama — 17
5. Fernleigh Manor — 23
6. Crisis — 27
7. Sadness — 30
8. Death — 35
9. The Sheltons — 38
10. Priscilla — 40
11. The Girls — 45
12. Nightmare! — 47
13. Christmas — 52
14. New Beginnings — 54
15. The Plot — 59
16. Happy Times — 63
17. The Will — 66
18. Victory! — 72
19. Percy Speaks His Mind — 75
20. Treachery! — 82
21. Davey Death — 85
22. Plans — 88
23. Goodbyes — 92
24. Cheapside — 95
25. The Park — 98
26. Romance — 102
27. Clandestine Meetings — 106
28. Surrey Gardens — 111
29. Lost — 116
30. Come Into My Parlour — 118
31. Nightmare — 123

32. Evil Lives Here 125
33. No Escape 129
34. Lanyard Lane 133
35. Arthur 139
36. Lilya 143
37. Talk 148
38. Middledene 153
39. Happier Days 156
40. Master Gregory 163
41. News 169
42. The Old Home 175
43. Churchyard 177
44. What Happened That July 185
45. Matthew Troubled 189
46. Lord Huckle 194
47. Where Evil Lurks 202
48. Sentencing 210
49. Mrs Quinn 216
50. Letters 221
51. Middledene House Revisited 225
52. Nottingham 230
53. Sherwood 233
54. Sherwood Abbey 237
55. Midwinter Journey 242
56. A Friend In Mr. Ellis 245
57. Where Were The Children? 248
58. Death Beckons 254
59. Bawd's Daughter 256
60. Where Is Caro? 259
61. Arthur In Hampstead 262
62. Mrs. May 264
63. Police 268
64. Arrest 271
65. Cab Stand 273
66. Justice Is Served 277
67. Seven Years Later 279

68. Reunion   289
69. Brother And Sister   292
70. Love Beckons   296
71. Confusion   299
72. Glennons Of Fernleigh   302
73. Going Home   307
74. Heartache   313
75. Meetings   315
76. Remaking Caroline   318
77. First Difficulties   321
78. Dinner Party   328
79. Arthur's Passenger   332
80. Eleanor   335
81. Love Rekindled   338
82. Future Plans   343
83. The Truth   346
84. Horace   350
85. Beezle Club   353
86. True Colours   356
87. Confession!   360
88. Joy   366
89. Back To Whitechapel   369
90. Nottingham   372
91. Matthew's Misery   375
92. New Prospects   380
93. One Wedding Leads To…   385
94. The Light Shines   387

Sign Up To Receive Free Books Every Week   391

1
EARLY DAYS

1 843

"Mama, why did you name me Caroline?"

The young girl was six years old and had already reached the age when she was wondering if her parents should have chosen another name for her, because she had heard enthralling names, and Caroline was not one of them.

"Why, would you prefer another name?" asked her mother with humour. "What name would you have liked, dear?"

The girl thought for a minute. It was a beautiful day, and mother and daughter were seated on the grass by the River Ferne, a little-known meandering stretch of water that ran parallel to the medieval Devonshire village of Fernleigh. They came here nearly every day in summer, as it was only a short walk from their house.

The bank was filled with meadow flowers. Daisies and cowslips dotted the green field in carpets of white and yellow, and in the shade under the trees, an army of bluebells danced in a lazy breeze. Bees buzzed about from flower to flower.

"I would have liked Victoria or Persephone," she said after a moment, pronouncing the last name with a lisp. She twirled her parasol.

Her mother laughed.

"You were named Caroline because I thought it a pretty name and your dear father did not mind what I named you. If you had been born later in 1837, I might have named you Victoria, but you arrived just before she became Queen."

"And Percy is named for Papa. I wish I remembered Papa." Caroline laid her parasol down. She was tired of holding it.

"He was a fine man, your Papa. We were very happy. When you're older, I will tell you the story of your Papa and me, and how we met."

"Please tell me now, Mama!"

"Oh, very well then! I was nineteen years old, at a ball, wearing a pale blue gown adorned with satin bows and lace, beautiful lace.I had gardenia blossoms in my hair. I saw this handsome dark-haired man on the other side of the room, talking with some ladies. I wished to know him. I was Miss Shelton then. He turned and I averted my eyes just in time, for he looked at me. My mother told me, *'that young gentleman likes what he sees.'* I looked up and smiled at him. Then, he contrived to be introduced to me, and asked me to dance. He bowed very gracefully. I consented, and when we danced, I knew immediately that he was the man for me. He must have felt the same, for he engaged me for the last two dances of the night, and at the next ball, the first two! When a young man engages you for the first two dances, you know he prefers you to every other girl at the ball. He was a handsome, kind man, and had a fortune. His family was well thought of, and no obstacle stood in our path. Both sets of parents were very happy. Our families visited each other, and everybody liked everybody else. Everything was perfect. We were married within three months. Percival was born after a year, and you two years after that."

"I want a blue wedding gown too, Mama, when I get married."

"There is no reason why you should not have a blue gown, my dear child, or any colour you like," said her mother with affection.

"Why does God let bad things happen, Mama?"

"I don't know, dear. It's called *'going through life,'* or so my old nanny used to tell me."

"I wish I remembered him, Mama. I'm sure he was the most handsome man in the whole wide world."

Her father had died when she was two years old. He was a keen sportsman and had been thrown from his horse, breaking his neck.

"He was, dear, but he is with God now, and we must get along without him. Now, where are Percy and Miss Beale?" she asked as the dressing bell sounded from their house, a handsome Georgian home set in its own copse of trees a short walk away. "Oh dear, you laid your parasol down, Caro, and I'm afraid you'll suffer from a headache. Put it up again, good girl."

Percy came running up then, a stick in his hand which he was swishing around like a sword. The Governess followed behind, and they went back to the house together, Percy and Caro running ahead. Mrs. Davey went to her chamber to get dressed, while Miss Beale and the children climbed another flight to get to the nursery.

"Miss Beale, what is your name?" asked Caroline. "Your Christian name, I mean. Mama says that everybody has a Christian name."

"It's Ophelia."

"That's a beautiful name, Miss Beale." Caroline determined to remember it with the other names she liked. The next doll she had would be named Ophelia.

There was excitement in a letter from London, for their mother's dear step-sister, Auntie Mary, had announced her engagement to Mr. William Barton.

"Are we to attend the wedding, Mama?

"Oh no, dear. London is much too far. But they will visit us soon after, I know."

The date was fixed. The newlyweds were to arrive on September 3rd.

"You must be on your best behaviour, and do not remark anything out of the ordinary," said their mother.

"What do you mean, Mama?"

Their mother hesitated. "Uncle William and Aunt Mary are not as well-off as we are," she said. "Their clothes and luggage may look a little less well than ours, but we must not say anything, and we must be very polite and make them welcome."

"Why are they poor, Mama?" asked Percy.

"They aren't exactly poor," was the reply. "He is a curate and you know, like Jesus, clergymen aren't supposed to go after money."

"Oh." The children had not known that.

"So that's why Reverend Pleasance hasn't got a carriage and why his guns are so old," Percy exclaimed.

"And Mrs. Pleasance wears old hats. And June wears Helen's clothes when she gets too big for them. June never gets anything new." Caroline chimed in.

"That's enough, children. These outside things don't matter, do they, Miss Beale?" She looked appealingly at the governess.

"It's what's inside a person matters. Riches mean nothing to God."

Mrs. Davey nodded in agreement.

The visitors arrived the following day, and Caro was quite surprised that in fact they looked quite well. She's been expecting her aunt and uncle to arrive dressed like the cottagers, but Aunt Mary had a smart hat and a stylish costume, and Uncle William looked just like a gentleman. They were smiling, friendly people, warm and joyful, especially Auntie Mary, who was very pretty with dancing eyes and a bright, effervescent personality, and who seemed to have an aura of warmth about her. Uncle William was more quiet, but very pleasant, and had a wry wit.

They had brought gifts for the children, a doll for Caro, and a toy soldier for Percy.

"Mary, you shouldn't have," scolded Mrs. Davey. "You're on your wedding-journey, and should not have to think of gifts and suchlike! What is that? For me? A lace collar! I shall attach it to my pink satin, for I have been very disappointed in the collar I have. It went yellow in the wash, and no amount of bleach can restore its colour. Oh thank you dear sister! And brother!"

"Thank you," Caro said very prettily when handed the little doll. She would be the smallest in her little family of dolls lined up on her chest of drawers. "She is small, so she will be the baby," she said.

"What are your dolls' names? I would so love to see them," Auntie Mary exclaimed.

"You will have to come upstairs, because I can't carry them all down, and Percy will not carry a doll for anything."

"Dolls!" said Percy with scorn, marching his toy soldier across an imaginary battlefield on the table.

There was only one awkward moment, and that was when the children learned that they lived in a place in London called Cheapside. Percy giggled, but Miss Beale gave him such a harsh stare that he immediately straightened his face.

"You must tell us what your wedding dress was like!" said Mrs. Davey of Mrs. Barton later on.

"Oh, it was a beauty! If I had crayons and paper, I would draw it for you."

Auntie Mary was accomplished in drawing, and the finished work drew exclamations of admiration from Caroline and her mother. It was a flowing, billowing gown, with layers of white tulle overlaying dove-grey satin, and the veil was long with a tiara of pink rosebuds.

"I think I'll get married three, no four, times to have wedding gowns," Caroline said with solemnity.

The women laughed, and she felt a little insulted.

"My dear, you will marry once only," said her mother, giving her an affectionate embrace. "When you find your true love! But you will have a ballgown when you're grown up, and it will be very pretty."

"I can't wait to grow up!" was the reply.

The visitors stayed a few days only. They had won the children's hearts with their easy manners and delight in everybody and everything they saw, and their willingness to take walks with them and answer endless questions. The children were very sorry to see them go, and they promised that when time allowed, they would come back.

3
UNCLE DAVEY

The children led quiet lives in their country village. Neighbours of their rank were not easily found, and Mrs. Davey was not sociable. There was an elderly uncle of her husband's, a retired Colonel named Edward Davey, who lived alone in a dull old house about four miles away. They paid him a regular visit, and since he expected to see the children, who were his heirs, they were brought along, though very reluctantly.

It was New Year's Day, and he had invited them to spend the day with him. Caro did not want to go.

"His house is dark and ugly. And he's so tall and his ears stick out, and his nose is like a pelican beak. You said so yourself."

"Oh dear! Did you hear me say that? But he's a good, generous man, Caro. We must pay our respects to him twice a year. He goes to the trouble of ordering ice-cream for you and Percy, because it is known that children are very fond of it."

New Year's Day was cold and foggy, and since Mrs. Davey had sold her carriage after her husband's death, Colonel Davey sent his equipage over for them. His home was deeper into the countryside, and the carriage was cold as they crossed a very exposed bridge where the wind howled, rocking them to and fro. They huddled together. Soon they came to the large iron gate, and the drive, a long tedious way to the front door of Fernleigh Manor.

"Mama, I'm glad we never have to spend the night, for it's like a horrid castle," whispered Caro, looking at the many turrets of the Restoration house. The fog gave them a ghostly, sinister appearance. She shivered in an exaggerated way, causing Percy to laugh.

The hallway was dark. Their uncle did not trust anything modern, and as yet no gas lamp had crossed the threshold of Fernleigh Manor. The butler held a candelabra aloft to show them into the drawing-room.

Their great-uncle rose to greet them. He was thin as well as tall; his clothes hung from him. The drawing room was almost as dark as the hallway, but at least a bright fire helped to light it up. The children were bidden to be seated on the sofa, and they answered his questions very politely. Was Percy's new tutor satisfactory? And he was learning Latin, was he? The Classics, nothing like the Classics, every boy should be versed in the Classics. And what was Caroline learning?

"Geography and History," she said solemnly.

"Where is Prague?" asked her uncle.

"I don't know, Uncle," she stammered.

"She is still within the British Isles," her mother came to her rescue. "She knows the principal cities of England, Scotland and Ireland."

"Good enough, good enough." Her uncle nodded, satisfied.

There followed several hours that, to the children, were boring. Uncle Edward always liked a private consultation with their mother, and they were sent out to roam the house, or outdoors if they liked. In summer, they found pleasure in exploring outdoors, for there was a nearby woods and a pond. A dry day in winter was an adventure too, but it was now raining outside. They opted to climb the stairs and peeked into the library and the bedrooms, all of which, except for Uncle Edward's large room, were covered in white sheets.

Something scrambled past Caro's feet and she screamed.

"There's no need to be affrighted, Miss." An old servant, known to them as Dorcas, appeared out of the darkness behind them, causing her to startle. The candle in her hand cast an eerie glow. "We've 'ad a bit of trouble with mice. I'll get the kitchen cat up 'ere later, and she'll do the job." She glided upon her way.

Percy had run down the hall and was halfway up the next staircase, wanting to know what was up there.

"There's just servants' rooms!" whispered Caro, fiercely, as she darted after him in an effort to bring him back.

"No, there's more! I bet Uncle Edward has an old chest hidden away, full of things from Waterloo," said Percy with eagerness. "Guns and uniforms and maybe things from the battlefield, souvenirs, French buttons and medals and everything!"He bounded out of sight, leaving her alone in the darkness. She began to make her way downstairs again. Surely Uncle Edward had finished speaking with Mother! Last summer, he had told her to engage a tutor, so Mr. Franklin had come to live with them. Uncle Davey paid for him.

She crept downstairs, but felt rather ashamed that she was so nervous when there was nothing to be afraid of. She did not believe in ghosts, not really. However, she thought, if ghosts were real, then Fernleigh Manor would be an ideal place for them to live.

She pushed open the door of the drawing room gently, but a draught immediately made the candles bend over with fury.

"Ah, come in, child," her uncle said with affability. She felt a little ashamed of being frightened of him and of his house. She came to her mother's side and sat on the arm of her chair.

"Where's Percy?" was the inevitable question. She shook her head. She wished she'd brought a doll. But Mama had thought that Uncle would think it a frivolity. He was very strange about many things, she said, but he was, she always added, a good man.

Percy reappeared some minutes later, his clothes somewhat rumpled. The bell was rung for dinner, and directly after eating they were taken home. Caro breathed freely again. She was so happy when the gate clanged shut behind them that she fell asleep on her mother's shoulder before five minutes were past.

4

MAMA

1847

It was June and time for another visit to Uncle Edward. Caro moped the day before, and Miss Beale lectured her mildly on it.

In the afternoon, Caro accompanied her mother to the garden. Roses were in all their glory, and lupins and marigolds made a blaze of colour along one side.

"Come on, Caro. Cheer up! Your uncle is very fond of you. He's just an old bachelor who isn't used to children. He's provided for you and Percy, you know, after he dies. I did not mean to tell you, but I supposed it's just as well, because now you can be fonder of him while he is here to appreciate it. He has made sure that neither you nor your brother will ever be in want. He has also covered my debts. You're old enough now, at eleven years of age, to know these things. But for Uncle Davey, we would not have been able to continue living here."

"That's kind of him, Mother." Caro admitted, as she took a scissors and snipped a white rosebud to add to her mother's basket.

"Go and pick some of the purple lupins," her mother said. "I'm going to get some foliage from the bower."

Caro bounded over to the sentry-like blooms, but before she reached them, she heard a short cry, and turned just in time to see her mother sway toward the rose-bushes. The basket fell from her arm, and the path was strewn with blooms.

"Mama!" she cried, running over to her. "What's the matter? You're so pale! Is it the sun? Harris! Harris!" she called out, summoning the gardener who was tending fruit trees nearby.

Soon, Mrs. Davey was being carried into the house by the gardener and his boy. She was placed on the sofa in the front parlour, and the curtains were drawn by Miss Beale, who had heard the commotion.

"What is the matter, Mama?" Percy was by her side, his face contorted in worry.

"I felt a weakness come over me." Mrs. Davey attempted to lift herself up, and failed. "I've had pins and needles in my feet for the last few days,on and off,but now, I cannot feel them."

"Mr. Heaphy, ask James to summon Doctor Farrell," Miss Beale ordered the butler. "And if he is not there, he will have to go to Johns Mills, to Dr. Glennon."

"Very well, Miss Beale," said the butler, who went at once to find the footman.

Dr. Farrell was attending a maternity case, and it was well over an hour before Dr. Glennon arrived. Caroline and Percy kept their eyes on the driveway and, when they saw the horseman, ran in to the parlour. It had been impossible to get Mrs. Davey upstairs. She could not walk.

The children were banished for the examination and went to the kitchen where Mrs. Lowry, the cook, gave them macaroons. The afternoon was turning into evening, and still the doctor was with their mother. Their patience running out, they went upstairs again to wait outside the door.

Suddenly, the door opened and Dr. Glennon emerged.

"Please, Doctor, what's wrong with our mother?" Caroline beseeched him.

"Will she get better?" Percy asked with anxiety.

James handed Dr. Glennon his hat and greatcoat. He looked at the two children before him. He had children, too. He could not tell them his diagnosis.

"Your mother needs peace and quiet," he said to them. "She will need to rest for a few weeks perhaps. Read to her, and be very good." He donned his hat and left.

When the children entered the parlour, they saw their mother's maid and Miss Beale whispering together by the window. Their mother appeared to be asleep.

The remainder of the day was the oddest in the children's lives, for they did not remember the day their father died. Mrs. Davey was carried upstairs by Mr. Heaphy and the tutor Mr. Franklin. She was conscious now, though it was an effort to speak.

Miss Beale and her maid Tennyson put her to bed, and then the children were remembered by their Governess.

"Come on, dears. Time for your dinner," she said crisply.

"Please, Miss Beale, I want to talk to Mama," cried Caro.

"Not tonight, dear. Tomorrow. She is not to be disturbed tonight."

The following morning, before Miss Beale was even up, Caro sped along the hall to her mother's room. Tennyson was there, sitting by her, and she looked up as Caro came in.

"Mama," Caro said, going up to the bed.

To her great relief, her mother opened her eyes and smiled.

"How are you, Mama?"

"I feel much better, Caro. Were you very anxious?"

"Yes, I was. And so was Percy. We were very worried."

Mrs. Davey was silent. Caroline suddenly remembered that the doctor said that there would have to be 'peace and quiet' so she kissed her mother's forehead.

"I'll come and see you later, Mother," she said fondly.

It was only upon her way back to her room that she remembered that today was to have been the day they were to have gone to Fernleigh Manor. She felt guilty that she felt happy about not going there, given that it was because her mother was ill.

5

FERNLEIGH MANOR

Two days later, Mrs. Davey was no better. She sat out on the chair with help, but her legs would not move, and she suffered a great pain in her back.

On the third day, Uncle Edward came in his carriage to see his niece-in-law. He went into the room alone except for Miss Beale and Tennyson, and when he emerged, instead of taking his hat and coat, he sat in the parlour.

Miss Beale summoned the children to the Nursery. Nobody used it much anymore, but it had a bright play area and sometimes the children spent rainy days there.

"Children, you heard the doctor say yesterday that your mother needed rest, and quiet?"

"Yes," they chorused. Miss Beale did not seem to know what to say next. She opened her mouth and shut it again, but then said, "Your mother wishes you to go to Uncle Edward for a little while. Until she is better."

"Your mother wishes you to go to Uncle Edward for a little while. Until she is better."

This was horrifying news to Caroline.

"But I'll be so quiet!" she said, bursting into tears. "I won't disturb Mother, I promise! I will be so good!"

"And I also," said Percy hotly. "We won't make a noise!"

"It's been settled. But if it makes you feel any better, Miss Caroline, I'm to go with you, and your tutor also, Master Percy. So it will as like home as we can make it. Now, I have to pack for both of you—"

"When are we to go?" asked Caro.

"Today. We will go in Colonel Davey's carriage, and he is anxious to be off, so he can dine at home. Now, go down and talk to him. Dry your eyes, Miss Caroline! It will only be for a few days."

"Are you quite sure?" asked Caroline.

Miss Beale did not reply, except to say, "I must pack."

She set off, and Percy and Caroline looked at each other in despair.

"I don't want to leave Mama either," Percy said. "She might need me to talk about things. I'm the man in the family, though I'm only twelve!"

They were allowed to say goodbye to Mama. She was in bed, her face drawn in pain, trying to move herself a little. It frightened both of them.

"Be good for Uncle Edward," she said. "He is good to you. Write to me every day, I will want to hear of your doings. I might not be able to write back for a while."

"But we're only going for a few days!" Caroline burst out.

Her mother said nothing. Beads of sweat stood on her forehead as she winced with a pain that she tried to keep from showing on her face. But the children were not fooled.

"Mama. You will get better quickly, will you not?" Percy asked her pleadingly.

"Yes, darling boy. As quickly as I can."

"That's enough," Tennyson ushered them away. They went downstairs slowly, reluctantly. They were very reluctant to leave, and not just because it was to the ancient and austere home of their uncle. They dared not put their fears into words.

6

CRISIS

Mr. Barton whistled softly as he entered his home at Cheapside. It was a very modest house at the older end of the churchyard, but since he had married, the curate's house had become a home. Mary adorned it. Mary, after four years, was still his sweetheart, and their little daughter Cathy was the light of their lives.

Their servant, Frances, took his hat and coat, and he went to find her in the parlour, where she usually was at this time of the day.

There she was, bent over her sewing for the baby, as he swung into the room and kissed her.

To his surprise, she did not return the embrace. Her eyes were swollen with crying.

"What's the matter?" asked her husband. Had he committed some spousal offence? Did he forget her birthday? No, that was next month. Their anniversary? Not at all, as that was three weeks ago. His examination of conscience ceased as she pulled a letter from her pocket and gave it to him.

"From your sister?"

She nodded, her eyes filling with new tears.

Dear Mary, I write in haste. I do not like to trouble you with my bad news, but it is such that I may not keep it to myself. I have been taken very ill. If you could find it in your power to come to me for a few days, I would so much appreciate it. I will then tell you all. The children are not here, for I have sent them to their father's uncle. They are well cared for there. Come as soon as you can.

Your loving sister, Catherine.

"What can it mean, William? She must be seriously ill to write thus! And the children sent from her! I must go at the soonest. Tomorrow. Thank goodness little Cathy is weaned. I could not go otherwise and take her to a house where there is sickness. Molly will see to her very well. Oh, what is wrong with my sister?"

She burst into a fit of weeping.

"Mary, she does not say that she is seriously or desperately ill. Do not fret, my love," said William, taking her in his arms, though he knew, from the urgent summons, that it could not be any different. He held her tightly. It was a long way from London to Devonshire, and he would send word to the church warden that he would not be in tomorrow, and he would conduct her there.

7

SADNESS

T he couple arrived in Fernleigh before dark the following day, and having disposed of her bonnet and cloak, Mrs. Barton hurried upstairs first to see Catherine. She was not prepared for what she saw, her sister, much thinner than she remembered, looking like a waif upon the pillows, wisps of hair on her forehead, her cap a little askew, betraying restlessness.

After warm and tearful greetings were exchanged, Mrs. Davey introduced her nurse, a good local woman the doctor had recommended.

"Tell me everything," Mary cried, nodding to the nurse to leave the room. She drew a chair up beside the bed. "What can ail you, Catherine? Your letter worried me, and I am not reassured by your appearance. You are thin, and very pale."

"It is this." Catherine said. "I have lost the use of my legs, and will soon lose the use of my arms, and so on, until my heart stops. I have a frightful pain in my back, going up and down my spine, like burning. I have consulted three doctors, and undergone the most thorough examinations. And Mary, you must be very brave. I am dying. I will not live beyond a few weeks more."

"But what is the matter? What did the doctors say?"

"They tell me it is a cancer." Her mouth contorted in pain as she shifted uncomfortably. "There is no cure. Dr. Glennon saw it once only before."

Mary sat with a numbness in her heart. This was the very worst news.

"I have made arrangements for the children," Mrs. Davey said then. "They are to live with Uncle Edward. You do not mind, sister, do you? That I haven't made you their guardian? You see, Percy is his heir, and-" she paused, struggling again. Mary wrung her hands, helpless.

"Is there nothing that can help you?" she asked in a despairing voice.

"There is laudanum over there,but I took it only a short time ago." Catherine sounded exhausted already. "I cannot have it by me, or I would might swallow it all! But about the children, Mary. I do not wish to separate them. So Caroline will live with Uncle Edward too. You don't mind, do you?"

"My dear sister, you know I would look after them as well as I could, if that was your wish. We are expecting another little stranger in the New Year, and though I would gladly take them," Mary did not know how to finish. Their house was not large. Their income was small. She found herself relieved that she and William did not have to take on more responsibility.

"It suits all, then. But I worry about Caro. She does not much like her uncle's house. But Miss Beale is with her. I hope she stays, and doesn't gad off and get married. Do write to Caroline, Mary, and take an interest in her, won't you? I worry about her. She takes fright at the least thing and is of a sensitive nature."

"Of course, of course," Mary soothed. She pushed the stray wisps of hair under the cap and righted it.

"Thank you," Catherine smiled. "I am so blessed to have a sister. I only feel for Caroline, that she does not. Who will be her friend? There is no friend like a sister."

"I have been greatly blessed, too, in you."

"How is little Cathy?"

"She is well, chirping little words, pulling herself up with her little chubby hands."

"Did you bring her?"

"No, I"

"It is not contagious. If you wish to stay longer than a few days, please send for her. Will you stay longer than a few days, Mary?"

There was an appeal in the voice.

"I will stay as long as you need me," she said.

The room was becoming rapidly dark.

"Percy and Caroline are to be sent for, in my last hours. I could not bear to have them watch me go like this, slowly and in pain. They are spared that."

There was a little silence.

"I think the laudanum is taking effect now," murmured Catherine. She shut her eyes. With shaking hands, Mary lit the lamp, then went to the window to draw the curtains. Hot tears spilled down her cheeks and would not be checked. She hurried from the room and ran downstairs to William.

8

DEATH

It was comforting to have Miss Beale about, and she was very kind, and thoughtful, and never became irate. Her uncle's house had not grown upon her at all, except that in summer, it was showing its best. Sunlight poured into the rooms, and the grounds were certainly beautiful. There were wild rabbits in the woods, and it amused her to watch them work their jaws rapidly on the leaves and grasses they chomped upon. They seemed to do nothing else!

She was there one September day, when she heard a sound behind her. She turned to see Aunt Mary there, her arms wide open for an embrace.

"Oh, it is good to see you, Aunt! How is Mama?"

"I have come to fetch you, Caroline. Percy is already in the carriage. Uncle Edward is on the box. Make haste."

The sunlight seemed to fade, the woods seemed suddenly darker, and the rabbit had darted away at the appearance of another human. Without even going to the house, she was bundled into the carriage and the horses began a swift run.

There was a peculiar quiet in the carriage. All was not well. She and Percy looked fearfully at one another. Again, they did not dare to voice the thought uppermost in their minds.

James opened the carriage door at their house. There was no robust greeting from the young man. He handed them out without saying a word.

Caroline looked at the familiar house with longing and love. A peculiar feeling in her heart told her not to hope that she would ever live here again.

"Children." Aunt Mary held her hand out to stop them as they surged eagerly toward the house. "I must tell you something. Your mother will have altered greatly since you last saw her. I tell you this so that you will not suffer a shock upon seeing her."

Percy and Caroline glanced at each other, in great fear now. All thoughts of running into the house were gone. They almost dragged themselves, so sick were their hearts. They longed to see Mama, but how would they feel when they did?

The room at the top of the stairs smelled of ether and other medicinal smells. There was a hush in there. The nurse sat by the bed. And was that their mother, lying within? How could it be, that this strange, whitened, bony-faced woman, her head hardly making a dent in the pillows, was their warm and rosy-cheeked mother! But it was her.

They called to her softly, but there was no response. They sat by her for hours. They held her clammy hand, which gave no sign of life. Only her breathing told them that she was alive. Caroline was with her when she fell asleep forever, peacefully, and any remaining colour drained from her lips.

She ran from the room and down the hallway, crying.

She and Percy were orphans.

9

THE SHELTONS

The funeral was a heartbreak for Mary and the children. One had lost a beloved step-sister, the others their most beloved mother. At the graveside, they did not notice a couple standing a little way off who seemed more interested in them than in the prayers said by the Reverend Pleasance.

After the funeral, lunch was served for the mourners in the house, the house which Percy and Caroline now felt was a cold, unfeeling place, and yet, it was home.

"What is to become of us now?" Percy asked, eating his game pie without his usual relish. "Why should we not live here with Miss Beale and Mr. Franklin? They would look after us, would they not?"

"It cannot happen like that, because if they were like a father and mother to us, I think they would have to marry." was Caro's reply. Her heart was heavy as she looked about the table. Everybody was talking, and some people were even laughing at something somebody said. How odd funerals were!

"Could we get them to marry, then?" Percy seemed serious.

"Oh, no. Miss Beale is too old to marry. Perhaps Auntie Mary and Uncle William will move here and look after us. I would like that best of all, wouldn't you? He is a clergyman and could build a church."

"I think it would be excellent," Percy said. "Shall we ask them? Caro, who are those people over there? They keep looking at us."

"I've never seen them before. Staring is rude." Caro said. As she looked up toward them, the woman in the high green hat averted her eyes.

10

PRISCILLA

"May we sit by you, Uncle Edward?" Mrs. Shelton asked heartily a little later, when he had seated himself in his drawing room by the tall ornate hearth.

"Of course," Colonel Davey said, rather surprised.

"What a tragedy, Uncle." Priscilla Shelton leaned toward him with an affectionate pat on the arm.

"So young, and the children are orphans now," added her husband Frederick. He was a man with keen eyes and a rather suspicious look, as if he thought the world was out to cheat him in some way. Edward had never liked him.

But he'd never liked his niece Priscilla either. He had not known her growing up, as she had spent her childhood in London. At the age of sixteen, she and her older sister had come to stay with him for a summer. For their sake he had opened up his house and arranged picnics and dinners where the girls would meet people her own age. He was not of a sociable nature, and he went out of his way for their amusement. The older girl was good-natured enough. But he was disappointed and ashamed of Priscilla, for she constantly spoke of how backward everything was in Devonshire, and she went out of her way to look superior, displaying fashions which to Edward's country mind were flashy, even immodest. He saw her as a rather petty-minded person who thought the servants were at her beck and call for every little matter. He had been glad to escort his nieces back to London at the end of the summer, but his hopes were dashed that Miss Priscilla would never appear there again, for Mr. Frederick Shelton, country bumpkin that he was in her eyes, had nonetheless taken her fancy. She returned the following year, with her mother as well as her sister this time, and the engagement was announced. He had to give an engagement party on the occasion, and he wondered how he was to endure such a relative living not three miles off. Happily, the Sheltons did not bother him very much, and he did not encourage the association. When they did meet, she struck him as a rather cold human being, perhaps disappointed in her choice to live in the country, away from 'all society' as she put it.

She was disinterested in everybody except her own spoiled children, two girls and a boy. She and Frederick Shelton were suited, for he was hard-nosed. He had a farm and numerous business interests besides.

"It is a great pity we don't meet more often, Uncle," she lamented to him now. "It's not good enough to meet only at funerals. It has been our fault entirely. I have been much taken up with the children. Little Henrietta is delicate. And Frederick, with all his business, never has a minute."

"You must visit whenever you wish," Uncle Edward said with as much warmth as he could muster. "It would be good for the children, especially poor Caroline, to see a female relative now and then."

There was a silence as this sunk in.

"You are taking in your great-niece and nephew?" Priscilla asked.

"Yes, of course. I cannot do otherwise."

"I should have thought that their mother's sister would be a more suitable person," Priscilla said in a careful tone.

"Mrs. Barton would be a great deal more appropriate for Caroline's care, but Percy belongs with me," he said. "And their mother was most anxious that they are not separated."

The couple digested this. Mr. Shelton did not speak very much, but his mind could be depended upon to make great conclusions. They said no more, but the couple burned to be alone where they could talk it over, so they took their leave soon after.

"I think it's clear what he means," Priscilla said, almost trembling with rage in the carriage. "*Percy belongs with me.* He has fixed on Percy Davey as his heir! I thought it was odd, at the graveside, how he kept the boy on one side, and the girl on the other. I think I knew it then."

"He's a capricious, funny old fellow, your uncle."

"How old is this Percy? What would you say, Fred? Older than our Howard?"

"No, Howard is taller, and must be the older."

"Then why should not our Howard be favoured? Why this Percy? I won't stand for it, no. Besides, I am his real niece. Catherine was only the widow of his nephew."

"How are we to prevent it, Priscilla?"

"We will change his mind. As yet, I don't know how. But we *will*."

THE GIRLS

The Sheltons lost no time. Priscilla decided that her daughters would be good companions for Caroline, and she brought the girls over one afternoon.

"Go outside and play," she said pleasantly to them. "You are cousins in a way, and will find lots of things to talk about."

The three girls went outside, but Caroline found that the sisters kept together, and that she was the outsider. They laughed and teased one another, and made private jokes, and altogether she thought Henrietta and Olivia quite rude. It was no pleasure for her, and when they returned, she went to her room while the girls went to join their mother, who was speaking with Uncle Edward.

That was only the first of many visits from the Sheltons. Mr. Shelton came once a fortnight, making himself very agreeable, and Uncle Edward seemed to enjoy his company.

I have misjudged the fellow, he said to himself. *He's a good enough sort.*

Another time, they brought their son Howard. He and Percy went off together to fish in a stream.

"We would so like for Percy to visit us," gushed Priscilla one day to Uncle Edward. "Perhaps he could come for a few days after Christmas?"

"Would you like to go, Percy?"

"Certainly, sir."

"It shall be, then."

Caroline did not like this development. She did not like the Sheltons and feared that Howard would be a bad influence upon Percy. Howard had a permanent smirk. And she had seen him throw stones at the little puppies and enjoy how they shrieked and scattered. She did not like Howard.

NIGHTMARE!

The evenings were getting shorter, and Fernleigh Manor took on its more menacing air. Caroline's room faced north and had a small, mullioned window, outside of which was a yew tree. When the wind was up, the branches of the yew beat the glass over and over in a relentless, sinister way, as if someone, or something, was trying to get in. Caroline lay in bed listening to it, trying to stop the thought that something out there was trying to provoke her, something that knew she did not want to be there and that wanted to punish her for it. Such thoughts, she knew, were not rational, but so much was not rational now. Her mother's death had left her floundering like a person about to drown. She felt afraid all the time, and she did not know of what. She felt sad, and nothing helped to make her happy. Miss Beale was kind, but not the type of person she could confide her inner thoughts to. Percy understood a great deal better. He was angry. He banged and kicked things. Not people or animals, just gates and logs that could not feel but that gave him relief.

One cold November evening the wind crashed about the house, and the yew tree kept up an endless nagging against the window. As Caroline was falling asleep, she felt herself unable to move. The sound of the branches became human voices. Grey shapes rushed to her from the window, and she tried to scream. No sound came. The shapes took on human form. They pressed down upon her, pinning her to the bed.

We have you now! They screamed. *You can't get away! You belong to us!*

She screamed and screamed, but nobody came. Where was Percy, whose room was next to hers? Could he not hear? Uncle Edward was farther down the hall, Miss Beale was upstairs. At any moment now, they would storm the room and chase these demons away. But they did not come, and the shapes had a grip upon her that she could not break.

God, help me! Jesus, where are You? Come and help me!

She tried to move again, and found that she could, a little. Feeling was returning to her arms and legs. She struggled to consciousness, and realised that she had been asleep, or caught somehow in that dim world between waking and sleep, trapped there. There were no shapes, no demons, nothing holding her down. The growling and screeching was only the rat-a-tat-tat of the branches and the wind. She sat up in bed, exhausted and trembling. She moved her arms and legs; all were working.

There was a presence in the room, but it was that of Love. She could not see anybody, but she knew it was there.

I'm with you, Love said. *I'm with you. Do not be afraid.*

She found great comfort in that presence, and her head sank back upon the pillows. She fell into a peaceful sleep soon after. When she woke up the following morning, the storm had passed and there was a serene quiet, even sunlight. She slipped out of bed and knocked on her brother's door.

"Did you not hear me screaming last night?" she wanted to know. "Why didn't you come and help me?"

He sat up, rubbing his eyes. "I didn't hear anything."

She asked Miss Beale, who had heard nothing either.

"It was just a dream," said the Governess, when she had listened to Caroline's story, which she related to her, for she was still very disturbed by it. "If you had screamed as you say, we would have heard it all over the house. But why did you not say before now that the branches are disturbing you?"

"Swap rooms with me, Caro," said Percy. "There's no tree outside my window. I shouldn't care if the branches hit the window all night long."

That seemed like a good solution.

Miss Beale felt it incumbent upon her to relate the incident to Colonel Davey, who was worried enough to send for the doctor.

"It is merely a hysteria," was the physician's opinion. "Brought on by the death of her mother. Young girls often experience the like. Their minds are prone to imaginative terror. It may happen again, but tell her that it is nothing really to be frightened of. She will not die from it. It is a sleeping paralysis. She is not insane, and no, she does not have her mother's disease."

Caroline was very relieved to hear this related to her later, and she heeded her uncle's command to her not to be frightened if it happened again. She remembered the presence of Love in the room, reflected upon it, cherished the memory, but told nobody. She did not think they would understand.

13

CHRISTMAS

Christmas approached, and Miss Beale proposed that the house should be decorated, if only for the children's sakes. The newspaper carried an article of how the decorations at Kensington Palace were to be enhanced, and families all over England were following suit. But decorations were an unheard of venture at Fernleigh Manor, and the housekeeper, Mrs. Erridge, was horrified. Decorations would set the house afire. They would all perish in their beds. She had to advise against it. A tree! Oh, not a tree. That was a German habit. She had great respect for the Prince Consort of course, but he shouldn't have introduced these foreign ways. He should have left them behind and adopted English ways. It would never last.

Miss Beale consulted Colonel Davey, who thought about it for a long time, before he told her that yes, but very limited decorations, some holly here and ivy there, that sort of thing, as was common when he was young. He disliked decorations. No tree. He had heard of this new thing and heartily disliked it. And he had heard of people sending Christmas Congratulation cards, with sketches of revelers stuffing themselves with puddings and drinking wine! Was there ever such a folly? Christmas was turning into a pantomime.

Miss Beale sighed to herself as she ascended the dark staircase. If the children had not been so recently bereaved, she would get another situation. She did not like this house. So draughty and old-fashioned! She was fond of the children. Caroline needed her. What a pity she could not go and live with her aunt!

She called Caroline to put on her cloak and bonnet and go to cut holly and evergreen boughs with her.

14

NEW BEGINNINGS

Colonel Davey was very pleased to see Frederick and Priscilla Shelton so attentive to the orphaned brother and sister. Percy went to them two days after Christmas, and stayed until the New Year, when the Colonel decided to accept an invitation to spend a day with the Sheltons when he and Caroline should go and fetch Percy back. Miss Beale had not been invited. In any case, she was due a holiday and decided to take it for the first two weeks of January. Caroline missed her. She did not like being without a female companion in the house. The servants were all old, apart from Millie the kitchen maid, but even if their ranks had allowed companionship, Millie never came upstairs.

She was not enthusiastic about visiting the Sheltons, but the thought of Percy returning with them cheered her. Uncle Edward was not a good conversationalist, and he was very happy to be quiet along the road, so that hardly a word was exchanged between them. But Colonel Davey's thoughts were busy, and they concerned his little great-niece. Caroline was very quiet and needed to be brought out of herself. Miss Beale was good with her, but a governess was an employee, free to go if she wished. She needed something more. Female relatives on hand. He would have a word with Mrs. Shelton.

The Shelton family lived in a large, well-maintained farmhouse along the road to Fernleigh village. They were the principal family in the immediate neighbourhood, a situation that had not been lost on Miss Priscilla when she first set her eyes on Frederick, who was of course the eldest son. It would not have been worth her while setting her cap at any of the younger. One of them had to enter the military, another went to sea, and the third was off in India at some humble customs occupation.

Brother and sister were happy to be reunited, and Caroline smiled at last. They contrived to have a few private words within a short time.

"I'm glad to be going home," Percy said in a low voice. "Howard is a bully and a cheat. He's cruel too. I don't like him at all."

"I missed you," Caro said. "The house is dull. Uncle Edward and I never talk at lunch or dinner. You're the talker."

Percy had a more outgoing nature, and at Fernleigh Manor he and Uncle Edward frequently spoke of the subjects he was learning. Uncle Edward used mealtimes to test his Military History, Algebra and Science. Percy did not feel in the least intimidated, as he was an intelligent boy and applied himself very well.

They could talk for only a little longer, as luncheon was served. Henrietta and Olivia giggled together as they always did. Caroline maintained a dignified silence, pretending not to mind.

"If I may have a private word with you, Priscilla," Uncle Edward said as the meal ended. "A little turn about the shrubbery, perhaps."

"Of course, Uncle, but it will not be too cold for you?"

"Not in the least. I walk a short distance after every repast. You and Frederick should do the same. It helps the digestion."

"I must remember that," Priscilla said, reluctantly getting her shawl.

"It is about Caroline," Uncle Edward said after they had left the house. "She is shy and needs to be brought forward. I could not help but observe during the luncheon, and indeed at other times, that your daughters tend not to include her in their conversation and games."

Priscilla bristled, but kept silent.

"My girls are so close in age, they are like twins," she said. "I shall remind them of their duties to other girls when they are in company with them."

"And, I would be so grateful if you could perhaps take Caroline under your wing a little too? It is a lot to ask, I know, but I worry about her not having any female about except for her governess."

It is a lot to ask, Priscilla thought with some anger. Caroline wasn't close kin.

"Would not her aunt be the best person? Perhaps she could go to her."

"No, for as I said before, Percy is to be with me. And they will not be separated. But I ask too much perhaps."

"Oh no, Uncle Edward, you do not. I will be a friend to her. And Percy, as you are so particularly fond of him, is not in any need of us, I would think, except="

"Except what?"

"If you should, oh,but you are healthy!" she pulled playfully at his sleeve. "You will be cross with me for speaking thus!"

"I am healthy now, but I may not be as the years go by. He will hopefully be in his majority before he must take over my affairs."

Priscilla swallowed quickly. Her heart grew hot with anger, but she did not allow her feelings to show.

"I'm sure that will be the case," she said, putting her arm in his. "And Caroline, why I shall invite her to stay this very night. You can send her clothes over."

"Would you do that, Priscilla?" he said with a smile.

"It is the least I can do! And I will have a stern word with my girls. They are just at a thoughtless age, you know, no malice at all is intended. They have hearts of gold."

"I knew I could depend upon you," said her uncle warmly. "I shall go and tell Caroline directly."

15

THE PLOT

U ncle Edward went in search of Caroline and found her wandering alone in the yard with the sheepdogs, with two puppies in her arms. She was surprised to see him.

"Is it time to leave already?" she asked hopefully.

"Almost time, but my dear Caroline," he said. "I have good news for you. I have arranged that you shall stay and have a little holiday here until Miss Beale returns."

To his dismay, her face showed no joy, only a confusion and dissatisfaction. She put the puppies down and they scampered off.

"Oh no, Uncle. Please don't make me stay here. I want to go back to Fernleigh Manor with Percy and you. Who will feed my pet rabbits?"

"My dear child, Percy will do that. You have to trust that I know what is best for you. I am aware that your cousins have not been the friendliest, but Mrs. Shelton assures me that they have just been thoughtless, and need a small reminder about their manners. Mrs. Shelton is most anxious that you stay with them. I got the distinct impression that she wishes to be a friend to you. I will have Lottie pack a suitcase and send it tomorrow morning. Now do not oppose me. You have to trust that the adults in your life know what is best for you."

She did not dare to put up an argument. Her uncle looked stern and unyielding, so she hung her head and said, "Yes, Uncle. If you wish it."

Inside, Mrs. Shelton called her girls away from their coloured paper and scissors to attend to her. She beckoned them to the parlour and shut the door. She looked so stern they thought that they were to be admonished.

"What is it, Mama? Have we done something wrong? You said we could have the gold paper as well as the red and blue."

"It's not about the paper, girls. You must attend to what I say. Caroline is to stay two weeks with us. No face, Henrietta, please. You are to be very good, attentive, and considerate towards her."

"Is it because she's an orphan?" asked Olivia, the more tender-hearted of the pair.

"Well, that too. But more than that, it is in your best interests, and for the sake of your brother Howard, that you are to be very nice to Caroline Davey."

"How can this affect Howard?" Henrietta asked, puzzled.

"Never mind. That is not for you to know. If Howard has good fortune, you will also."

"Are you going to tell Howard to be nice to her too?" asked Olivia. "He calls her stupid and dull."

"I will have a chat with Howard also," their mother said. "Now, go. Find Caroline, and offer to show her how to cut paper into figurines or whatever it is you are doing."

"All right, Mama." The girls left, still mystified, but obedient.

Howard was next on her list. He cast his eyes to the ceiling but listened to her lecture. He promised to be polite and kind to their cousin, and not to tease her.

She had not time to tell her husband before the Davey carriage departed, so he looked in amazement at Caroline when she came out without her bonnet and cloak and waved her Uncle and brother goodbye.

The children went off on their various amusements, and Mr. Shelton turned to his wife for an explanation. He was amazed.

"Goodness, woman, your mind works in genius ways. Get on his right side! And what then?"

"You must do your part, Frederick. You must visit often, and talk business, and sooner or later he will tell you of his plans. You must say that you would be the best person to take care of the interests of the Davey orphans. You will work on him and change his mind. I have hope to believe it will not take very long at all."

16

HAPPY TIMES

Caroline was surprised to find that she settled in very well with the Sheltons. Hetty and Olivia were attentive, showed her all over the farmyard, took her to all their secret places in the orchard and along the stream, and made themselves very agreeable. Aunt Shelton was fondness itself. She indulged her, asked her what she would like for dinner, what her favourite dessert was, and made her a present of a red shawl. Caroline lectured herself for her former dislike of the family. They were kindness itself. Uncle Shelton always had an indulgent smile for her and gave her a pony to ride while she was with them. Howard taught her how to ride. She slept in the girls' bedchamber in an extra bed pushed in there. It was a bright, happy room with colourful wallpaper and furnishings of the girls' own choosing. She tried on their gowns and bonnets, and they tried on hers. They chatted long into the night, laughing and joking, and shushing each other because they were supposed to be asleep. She got dirty running around the wet yards with the dogs and got straw in her hair sliding down the bales of hay in the barn. She knew the barn cats by name and carried them around until they inevitably wriggled free. She was tired every night, slept very well, and enjoyed every moment she spent there.

The two weeks flew and soon she was waving goodbye, her arms full of presents to take home. A pair of knitted slippers for Uncle Edward. A catapult for Percy. Blancmange and preserves made from the fruit of the Shelton orchards.

They have certainly risen to the occasion, thought Uncle Edward as he tried on his slippers. *All it took was a little effort on my part. Caroline looks happy and blooming. I should have been more friendly down through the years. But it is not too late, it is not too late.'*

. . .

"Uncle Edward, Mr. Shelton said he will call upon you next Sunday," Caroline was saying.

He was positively getting to like the man!

"I'm glad they were nice to you," Percy said. "They didn't spoil me as much. But then you're a girl, and girls are spoiled."

He ducked as she threw her bonnet at him. He threw it back and they laughed.

Uncle Edward looked over at them with indulgence. Having children about the house had its compensations. There was never any dullness. He felt that his own heart had enlarged and expanded when he had made room for them in his home. He felt very pleased that he had made the correct decision to make Caroline stay with the Sheltons for two weeks.

17

THE WILL

As the months passed and the attentions of the Sheltons increased, Colonel Davey began to think about his Last Will and Testament. He was not very rich, but the house and park was clear of debt and he had a tidy sum in the bank. He had left all to Percy, with the exception of a good sum for Caroline when she turned twenty-one, and now it did not seem fair. He realised that Priscilla, his niece by blood, had more claim on him than they. But the Davey children had nothing, and nobody, and that made him reluctant to alter his will.

Mr. Shelton, though spring on the land was busy, still found time to visit. He was often accompanied by Mrs. Shelton and the children. It became a regular Sunday outing for them to visit him, or for him and the Davey children to visit them, and he enjoyed the visits greatly. Priscilla had greatly improved in manner and demeanour.

As the year wore on and summer became autumn, an old wound he had received at Waterloo began to disturb the old man. It was in his shoulder, near the neck, and he had been lucky that the surgeon had been on hand to stitch him up immediately, but had not been able to remove every piece of metal. There was, he had said, a piece dangerously near the spinal cord, and it was better to leave it alone. Now and then, Colonel Davey felt a pain from it but had thought little of it as a younger man. He had made his peace with it for forty years.

But old age was catching up. His neck and shoulders had been ramrod straight, perfectly in line, even after his injury. But the years had caused a shift, and now his neck was bent. And with that curve came a pressing pain from his old wound.

He confided in Frederick Shelton one October evening when Frederick rode over to see him. Mr. Shelton said that he had to see the doctor without delay. Frederick thought it a most serious matter. And as it was a question that only a good friend could have the freedom to ask, someone with his best interests at heart, did he have his worldly affairs in order?

Mr. Davey did not immediately answer.

"I'm not sure. You see, Fred, the Daveys' children's mother was like a daughter to me, perhaps because she always lived near. And I made everything over to Percy. Now, I am not so sure I did the right thing."

Mr. Shelton looked at him keenly. "You have doubts, Uncle?"

"I have doubts. I rather think there are more claims upon my estate than I had thought. I would not like to do anybody a disservice. Not the Davey children, nor my own niece Priscilla."

"Priscilla. Of course." Frederick tapped his pipe against the hearthstone. "But it is your money, and your choice, Uncle Edward." He said this in a tone that betrayed only a tinge of censure.

"You know," he added, after a minute's silence. "Priscilla and I are uncommonly fond of the Davey children."

"I have seen that, and it pleases me."

"They are young, very young."

"Very young if I were to die soon, you mean?" Uncle Davey smiled a little wryly.

"Sir, I do not like to think of that. But in the case of such an unfortunate event, it would probably fall upon me and my wife to look into their affairs and see how they are situated, as we are on hand. My thought, sir, is this. If they were to be alone in the world, who would look after them? Who would advise them? With whom would they live?"

"With whom, indeed. My will was drawn up before their mother died, so that is a question I did not have to consider."

"If that were to happen, Uncle, be assured that Priscilla and I would welcome them into *our* home."

"Would you?" Uncle Edward looked quickly at him, in a little surprise. "They do have an aunt and uncle in London, you know. I understand they are not rich, though he has lately got a parish, but if the children were provided for, they could live with them."

"A very good prospect, sir. How long is it since they have met?"

"Oh, not since the funeral of their mother. It is far, you know. They write back and forth. Perhaps when the railway comes to Fernleigh, but may it never come! How I detest how they are cutting up the countryside for those ugly linked carriages! I beheld one once, from a bridge, and it made a tremendous racket coming along, and then slid underneath me, and I could not breathe for the smoke, and the monstrosity put me in mind of a giant snake."

Frederick was afraid that his mind had wandered from their discussion, so he gently brought him back to it.

"Indeed, they are ugly things. And speaking of smoke, London is very unhealthy," he remarked. "Children who are used to country air do not do well in cities. You have heard, I'm sure, of the bad air and the cholera outbreaks."

"I was in London once only, and could not wait to get out of it," remarked the old man. "I would face ten more Waterloos before I would make another journey to London."

Mr. Shelton hurried to say what he had to say next, before the conversation wandered back to the Battle of 1815, as it seemed to do with all old men who had fought there. He had bravely endured the account of Colonel Davey's part in defeating Napoleon Bonaparte several times now.

"If, God forbid, the children should need a home again, we should like to offer it. Priscilla is uncommonly fond of them. They are all of an age with ours. We would do our best for them. I say that so that you can be at ease."

"I thank you. You and Priscilla are good-hearted people. I hope it shall not be for a long time, but something has altered in my neck. The doctor says I should be prepared. If this thing pierces my spine at last, I could be finished."

Frederick offered a silent prayer of thanks to a vague god he worshipped, which was mammon, though he was very unaware that he worshipped mammon at all. He thought he was a Christian. He went to church every Sunday, but as soon as he stepped outside the door he did not think of the One True God again until the following Sunday.

"That is dreadful news, Uncle, but doctors are often wrong. Don't think on it. You will have another twenty years of health."

"I doubt it." Mr. Davey seemed to sink into a reverie, wanting no more talk, and his nephew-in-law knew it was time for him to depart. He hoped he had achieved something. He bowed and took his leave.

18
VICTORY!

Mr. Shelton was back the following week, and again, the men smoked tobacco together in the drawing room after the children had said goodnight.

"I have been thinking," Mr. Davey said slowly. "About what we discussed last week. I am now of the opinion, the decided opinion, that I must alter things from the way they presently stand."

Mr. Shelton nodded with solemnity. "Yes, Uncle?"

"I would like to do the right thing by my niece."

Mr. Shelton nodded again, with more solemnity.

"That is most generous of you, Uncle." He waited, but Mr. Davey said no more.

"I can put your mind at ease, Uncle, that I and my wife="

"Could I make you and Priscilla their guardians?" he asked suddenly.

"Of course, Uncle! We would be honoured. However, it is to be hoped that they will be out in the world before that lamentable day comes, and they might not need us."

Mr. Davey made no reply.

"I will alter my will, then, Frederick. This is my plan." He took a sheet of paper out of his pocket and handed it to him. Frederick held it near the candle and strained to read it.

"Priscilla! All to Priscilla? That is very generous, Uncle Edward."

"Not at all. It's the right thing to do. She is my nearest relation. I had thought of leaving all the children an equal amount when they come into their majority, but that is too much thinking for an old man like me, whether to leave the boys more than the girls, and how much, and so on."

Mr. Shelton's heart was beating so fast he thought it would burst out of his chest.

"You give me your word you will see to Percy and Caroline," said Mr. Davey, fixing his eye, taking the paper back from him, and folding it up again.

"I give you my word, sir."

"Priscilla's share, of course, will be yours in law. You will always be good to my niece?"

"We are the happiest couple in England as it is, sir, but if it puts you at ease, I will promise."

Mr. Frederick Shelton mounted his horse that evening and thought himself the cleverest man in England. He had control over the entire Davey estate when Mr. Davey should pass away. When would that be? Guilt stabbed his heart at the evil thought.

Priscilla was overjoyed.

"I would not have promised him that the children could live here," she said. "But it does not matter. Oh how clever you are, Fred! I hope he does it now, as it's no good if he doesn't get the lawyer. You must visit in the next couple of weeks or so, to make sure."

Just before Christmas, Fred was very happy to report that the will had been altered, and he came home with the happy news.

PERCY SPEAKS HIS MIND

The following night, Colonel Davey closed his book early, sent Caroline to bed, and told Percy that he wished to speak with him.

"Percy, I am an old man. You are fourteen years old, and when I leave this earth, you must take care of your sister."

"Of course, sir. I will always be responsible for Caroline until she gets married."

"My remaining days on this earth may be short in number, Percy. I want to inform you of the arrangement and provision I have made for you and Caroline."

Percy did not know what to say. Should he tell his uncle that he would live to a hundred? Did not people say something of that sort?

"I hope you are wrong, sir, about your days on earth being short," he burst out at last.

"I am not wrong, Percy. I feel…but never mind. This time next year, I shall be in Eternity. Not a word to Caroline. She is easily upset and dislikes changes. She's also a bit fond of me, I hope, and could be distressed to hear that I have not long to live."

"She is, sir, and she would be distressed." Percy wasn't sure, but his uncle appeared to expect an affirmation.

"Good, good. Well, this is what I have arranged. You and Caroline will go to live with Mr. and Mrs. Shelton. How do you like that?"

"It will be well, sir." Percy had also benefited from the Shelton campaign to show Uncle Edward that they loved the Davey children, but he had one doubt about it, and that was something Howard had said to him in a quarrel one day.

"Good. They are to be your legal guardians."

"Yes, sir. I am very grateful that you thought of us."

"Of course, boy. Now what would you like to do with yourself? The Army perhaps? Mr. Shelton will see that there's money for a commission. Or you might prefer the Law. Again, it will be provided for."

Percy considered. It seemed that Mr. Shelton would be in charge of all their money. He supposed that it had to be that way. He was too young to be in charge of it himself. He felt a little cloud of suspicion drift over him after what Howard had said to him.

"That will be all then, Percival. I shall turn in early myself, I think."

Percy said goodnight and went upstairs. In his room, he sat on the bed and thought deeply. Something sounded wrong. What was he to do?

The following day, he asked for a private interview with his uncle in the library where the old man spent his mornings. It was dark and gloomy like the rest of the house, but his desk was by the window.

"It concerns what we spoke of last night," he began. "When my mother was alive, she told me something."

"She did?" Uncle Edward was taken aback.

"So I, for my own and for Caroline's sake, should like to know if that still stands. Am I your heir, sir?"

Edward was speechless. He had no idea that the boy's mother had told him that he was his heir. This put him in a very awkward situation indeed. The boy stood before him, a good, honest boy, frank and open, and expecting the truth.

"I am afraid that things have altered," he admitted with some nervousness, which was uncharacteristic of him. "Your deceased father was my next-of-kin, and I did make you my heir, with a view to your mother having the management of the money until you came of age. But when she passed on, my next-of-kin was Mrs. Shelton, my other niece. So I made her my heir, or heiress, outright. She and Mr. Shelton will be generous to you."

"I see," said Percy. He bit his lip.

"What is the matter, Percival? I don't want to detect greed or avarice in you. I think more of you than that. The Sheltons have promised to do well by you."

"Yes, sir." Percy's brow furrowed in a frown. "I'm not greedy, sir," he said quickly. "But are, I think."

"Percival, what are you saying? Think well before you accuse good people of such a vice!"

"Forgive me, sir. It's something Howard said to me when we quarreled once. He said that he did not like having to be civil to me all the time. I said 'And why do you have to be civil to me?' and he replied, 'So as to get on the right side of Uncle Davey, you fool.' But I thought no more of it, so I never told you of what he said. That's it, sir."

Mr. Davey shrank back in his big leather chair. He uttered an oath to himself. He had gone deathly pale.

"Oh now I see it, now I see it!" he groaned, his head in his hands. "What a fool I was! I was taken in!"

He did not move, and Percy moved closer to him.

"Uncle!" he cried.

His uncle raised his head. To Percy's relief, he spoke.

"Ring the bell, ring the bell!" the old man blurted out. Percy darted to do as he was told.

"Get me my pen! The inkwell, fill it up, as it's nearly dry! Bring some paper!"

He dipped the pen in the ink with shaking hand and wrote a note in a quick, spidery scrawl.

"Tell Giles to go to Johns Mills directly and give this to my attorney-at-law, Mr. Alton. If he's not available, then another. He is to bring an attorney back. Make haste." He got to his feet and swayed a little, and Percy darted forward to support him lest he fall to the ground. He guided him to sit again in the chair.

"Sir, I think you need the doctor," said Mr. Boone, who had been passing and heard the unusual shouts.

The doctor was in Fernleigh, much nearer, within walking distance, so another footman was dispatched for him while Giles was ordered to take the carriage out, but he returned saying that an axle had broken, and wouldn't be fixed for an hour or so. He was directed not to wait, but to take one of the horses into town.

The commotion alerted the rest of the house, and Caroline sped to the Library. She saw her uncle holding his head, his eyes glazed, and the butler persuading him to retire to bed to await the doctor.

Caroline was deeply concerned. Though always in awe of her Uncle, she had seen that he had a good heart and had grown fond of him. He smiled feebly at her when she laid her hand on his sleeve and asked if he was all right.

"I am not, but as soon as I have seen Mr. Alton, I will be at peace."

The doctor was there within a half-hour, and Percy and Caroline sat on the steps of the staircase while he examined their uncle.

"And what will become of us if poor Uncle dies?" she asked Percy in whispers.

He decided to tell her all. She was dumbfounded.

"But that's horrible. Percy, I love Aunt Priscilla and my cousins. She didn't love us just to get Uncle Edward to change his will. That's not fair."

"We shall see," was his reply. "Alton is to void it, or nullify it, or something like that. I hope he comes soon."

Caroline wrapped her arms around her knees. "I can't imagine Aunt Priscilla and Uncle Fred being like that," she said. "I just can't. People are not that deceiving, are they?"

20

TREACHERY!

Giles had travelled only a mile in the direction of Johns Mills when he saw a smart red brougham approach. Mrs. Shelton, overjoyed at the promised change in her circumstances, was driving herself to see her benefactor. She also wanted to examine the house, her house, with a new eye. Olivia was beside her. She recognised Giles and hailed him.

"What is your hurry, man?" was her shout. He slowed.

"I have to ride to Johns Mills. The master has taken bad and he wants to see his attorney," said Giles. "I would beg you not to delay me. It's urgent."

"Taken bad!" exclaimed Mrs. Shelton. "Is Mr. Shelton ill?"

"Yes, ma'am. John is gone for the doctor and I'm off to-"

"Yes, I heard, I heard. What can he possibly want withhis attorney? What happened? I must know, Giles. What happened?"

"It's like this, ma'am. Young Master Davey went to speak with him, then he took ill and said he wanted to see his attorney directly."

Mrs. Shelton's mind worked very quickly.

"You won't make good time on that old horse," she said. "Our dear little Vulcan is keen for a good run today. Look at him. He hates to be still. I will relieve you of your duty, and my daughter and I shall go to Johns Mills directly, and bring him back."

Giles hesitated.

"Are you sure, ma'am? I have strict instructions."

"Of course I'm sure! I will brook no discussion. Go back to the house, and if anybody gives you trouble about it, just tell them what happened, and I will take the responsibility."

"All right, ma'am. He said to give him this note, ma'am."

She took it from him.

Giles turned the horse about and rode back toward Fernleigh Manor.

Mrs. Shelton turned her carriage around and set off.

"All the way to Johns Mills, Mama! We'll be at least an hour and miss luncheon."

Her mother said nothing. When the turn came for Johns Mills, she rode straight past it.

"Mama, what are you doing? Johns Mills is that way!"

"We are not going to Johns Mills, Olivia. Ask no questions, and tell nobody what has transpired this morning. I suppose you will tell Henrietta though. It must not go outside our immediate family."

"But when Uncle Davey finds the attorney doesn't arrive, what then?"

Her mother said nothing. The horses clipped along until their farm came into view, and her mother told a farmhand to find Mr. Shelton directly. She opened the note.

Mr. Alton. The <u>new will</u> I made is now void. I am burning it. Please will you burn your copy? And come to me <u>today</u>! If you cannot come, send Sanders! Quickly. No time to be lost! Yours, etc., Edward Davey

DAVEY DEATH

The day wore on. The doctor came again, stayed an hour, gave orders for his care to the housekeeper and went upon his way.

Uncle Davey lost the power of speech. But his eyes burned with anger and he plucked the bed covers with impatient fingers.

The attorney did not come.

"Are you quite certain, Giles, that Mrs. Shelton said she would go for the attorney?" Boone asked the footman for the third time as he paced the hall, stopping to look out the window every now and then.

"As sure as my dead grandmother is up in the churchyard, Mr. Boone. I looked back and saw 'er turn the team about to set off."

Boone continued to walk the hall with impatience, checking his watch at intervals. The axle was mended, and he took it upon himself to go to Johns Mills at about four o'clock.

While he was gone, Mr. Davey's condition became worse. Caroline and Percy stayed with him. Percy, too, kept a vigil at the window in between sitting by his Uncle.

"She never went to Johns Mills," he said in an undertone. "We are done for, Caro."

She frowned at him, in case her uncle could hear. Mrs. Erridge came in and out, as did Miss Beale.

About six o'clock, Colonel Davey breathed his last. A half-hour later, Mr. Boone returned with Mr. Alton.

Giles was sent to Shelton Farm to inform the family. He puzzled as to what had happened that morning. When he reached there, he noted that his news was received without any emotion by the Sheltons. No exclamation of grief, not a tear.

"They were expecting the attorney all day," he ventured, in an accusatory tone.

"I was diverted upon urgent business, Giles. Not that it's any of your concern." Mrs. Shelton went to a vase on the mantel and drew out a banknote. "This is for your trouble."

"No, thank you, ma'am." He turned on his heel.

"If you wish to stay on at Fernleigh," she said in a meaningful tone.

"Perhaps I do not, ma'am," he replied. "Mr. Boone will give me a good reference."

The funeral was two days later. After the other mourners had departed Fernleigh Manor, the house settled into an eerie silence. Aunt Priscilla and Uncle Frederick sat in the drawing room, very quiet. Perhaps they were feeling guilty. Percy paced back and forth outside the window, glaring in. He did not seem to want to be under the same roof as the Sheltons, and he avoided them.

Caroline longed to be comforted. The last few days had brought back her mother's death to her in great force. But nobody paid any attention to her. Only Olivia had put her arms about her before being dragged away on a walk by Henrietta. Miss Beale had stayed by her side until they had returned to the house, and she had not seen her since.

At last, the silence was broken.

"We've arranged you should visit your relations in London," Mrs. Shelton said at last. "You would like to see your Aunt Mary, would you not?"

"Oh, yes!" Caroline lifted her tear-streaked face.

"Uncle will take you there tomorrow then."

"I cannot." Mr. Shelton said. "Biggs is coming over to look at the grey horse. Robert can take them."

"For how long will we remain in London?" Caroline asked.

"For as long as you wish. Forever." Aunt Priscilla said. "I am sure you would much prefer to live with your mother's sister. She is the proper person to take care of you, more than me. There's no need to stare at me like that, Caroline. We have put ourselves out for you for long enough."

Caroline was aghast at the cold expression on Aunt Priscilla's countenance. Was Percy right? She saw him now, outside the window, looking in angrily. Her heart sank. What an utter betrayal! What treachery! She could not speak.

"Why do you not go upstairs now, and pack?" Mrs. Shelton suggested. "And tell Percy to do the same.

You are not to go into any of the rooms, by the by. Nothing in this house belongs to you."

While Caroline was in her room folding her clothes, she heard Miss Beale's hurried footsteps go over and back, over and back, on the floor above. She was busy too. She called to Percy and they ran up the stairs to her and knocked on the door. She invited them in. The room was strewn with her clothes and belongings.

"I've had marching orders," she said. "I'm to go tomorrow, and Mr. Franklin has already left. The new mistress would not tell us what was to become of you and your brother."

Caroline told her. The governess was relieved.

"Your aunt and uncle are the best people to take care of you," she said.

"Mr. Franklin left without saying goodbye." Caroline said.

"He had words with the new master," Miss Beale replied, taking a pair of boots and stuffing pairs of stockings inside them. "Do you see what I am doing? A great saving on space," she added.

"Isn't there anything you can do to get our inheritance for us?" Percy asked with desperation.

She shook her head.

"There is nothing, Percy. What is done is done. The last will your uncle made is the valid one."

"It's so unfair," he muttered with anger. Miss Beale could only look upon them sympathetically.

"I have to start anew with another family," she said. "That will not be easy, especially since you and Miss Caroline and I, and Franklin the tutor of course, have all gotten along so well."

"I'll miss you, Miss Beale!" Caroline said. "You've been with us for as long as I can remember!" Tears stood in her eyes.

"I will miss you too," Percy said. "You were our last link with Mama. Now, there's nothing."

"Children, if I may call you that, for you are still young, you have each other. And try not to brood on your misfortune too much. Your lives are before you. Give me your aunt's address and I shall write to you."

"Would you, Miss Beale?" Caroline's eyes lit up with hope.

GOODBYES

Miss Beale had her reference. It was a very good one, and she tucked it safely inside her reticule. She had her month's pay in lieu of notice. Now she would speak her mind to Mrs. Shelton.

"Miss Beale?" Mrs. Shelton was arranging the drawing room. She'd had the footmen remove Colonel Davey's pipe rack that always stood on the mantelpiece, and his beloved old chair was being carried out to be dumped in an old barn.

"The Davey children, Ma'am. I believe they are to leave today, and I would be at ease if I knew what arrangements have been made for their future. Their mother would wish me to ask this. I am sure of it."

"It's none of your business, Miss Beale."

Mrs. Shelton turned her back.

"You and the children are to travel together to Johns Mills in the carriage," she said. "What you do from there is your own business. I have arranged that one of the men will escort them to Town. There. Are you satisfied now?"

"No, I am not, but I can see it's useless to enquire further. Good day, Madam."

At Johns Mills, Miss Beale was to await the stage which would take her to Exeter, while the children were going in the opposite direction. To their surprise, she drew them to her and kissed their foreheads.

"Remember one thing," she said. "You can think yourself unfortunate all your lives long, or you can count your blessings. And we have blessings. You have health and education. You are full young for such troubles, but there are people worse off than you. Keep your Faith no matter what. What comes to my mind is that *'Gold is tested in fire.'* You are young for such lessons, but we may not meet again."

"I do not care for fire," said Percy crossly.

"Nor me, but thank you, Miss Beale." Caroline said, and though Percy set his lips firmly, he held out his hand to shake hers. They watched her board the stagecoach She gave one last wave, and a few minutes later it clattered away, around the corner and out of sight. They both fell silent.

"Remember my bad dream?" Caroline said suddenly. "I was being attacked, murdered. And then I felt God's love come over me and comfort me."

"Yes, I do. What of that?"

"Now we've been attacked, in a way, haven't we? We've been robbed. But God is still with us and He will help us, won't He?"

"I suppose so," he said. "But I do think Uncle and Aunt Shelton might have given us some money."

The following evening, Aunt Mary was astonished to find the Davey children standing upon the doorstep looking lost and forlorn, their bags by their side. Invited in without delay, and made to feel welcome, they soon apprised her of the whole story.

"And you came quite alone, except for the servant?"

"Yes, Auntie."

Mary thought it extremely rude of the Sheltons not to have come themselves. Robert had conducted them all the way, and then had turned around at the door and left for an inn.

Mr. Barton was rector now of St. Saviours and they had moved to the house in the church grounds. It was bigger than the curate's house. She would have to do some quick rearranging, but it was imperative that the children feel welcome, so she fussed over them, gave them something to eat, and asked them about themselves. There were two little Bartons now, and the children hung about their mother's skirts, examining the two strangers. The housemaid was summoned to make up two spare rooms, and they were shown to what was to be their new home for the remainder of their childhoods.

The house was comfortable and well-maintained. The outside was grey stone and covered in ivy, which Caroline thought very pretty. The only aspect Caroline did not like was that her room looked out upon the graveyard, but she decided quite firmly that she was not going to be unnerved by that.

Uncle William was very gracious and welcoming, but later that night, the children did not hear the conversation between him and his wife. She was seated at the dressing table. taking pins from her hair.

"Nothing, no money at all?"

"Percy volunteered the information himself. It was quite surprising. I had the whole story. They are supposed to provide for them. Instead, they just sent them away."

"Preposterous!" he exclaimed, walking up and down the room. "They cannot get away with this, if it is true. First, I will write to this Shelton fellow. If I don't get a satisfactory answer, I will put it into the hands of a lawyer. Thank God I got a parish, Mary."

"We will manage, won't we, Will? Even if they live with us? Even if the Sheltons provide nothing? Percy can help you with the church, and Caroline will help me with the children."

He laid his hands on her shoulders and kissed the top of her head.

"We can't turn them out on the street. We'll manage."

Mrs. Barton was gave birth to another child, and Caroline found herself busy as she took over the household duties during her recovery. At fourteen, she was growing pretty, with dark hair and large dark eyes, and had a ready smile for everybody. She felt happy at her aunt's. London was different than Devonshire, but it was exciting also. There were fine streets and parks and fashion and everything modern. She did not miss Fernleigh. Her aunt's house was bright and merry and noisy with the chatter of children, and Auntie Mary was happy to have her about, and told her so many times. She was happier that she had been at any time since her mother was alive.

Percy had been enrolled in a school nearby, as Uncle William thought it a shame for him not to continue his education. It would give him better prospects. The Sheltons had grudgingly provided a sum of money to cover it, but only after repeated demands from Mr. Barton and his lawyer, and they had also handed over one hundred pounds for Caroline when she should turn eighteen. Percy had taken an avid interest in all matters legal. While he did not blame his Uncle Davey, he saw that he had been worked upon in an insidious way. He was resolved to become apprenticed to a lawyer's office and was determined to work hard. He planned to become competent in solving every tricky and tangled legal case to be found in London, helping people get their rightful inheritances, and exposing people like the Sheltons. And if Uncle Davey was watching from above, he could be at ease knowing that Percy had done all right for himself.

Caroline often took the two older children out for a walk. There was a little park nearby with bushes and flowerbeds and other children running about. She allowed them to roam free, As long as she could see them, she was sure they were safe. There was a little hillock in the park, and the children used to run up to the top and roll themselves down. She would watch them from the bottom.

One day, little Cathy rolled down and started to howl at the bottom of the hillock. Caroline darted up and ran to her. Cathy had rolled onto a sharp stone and was bleeding from her hand.

"Oh, Cathy!" cried Caroline, taking the bleeding hand in hers, looking at it with horror. She fished in her pocket for her handkerchief, but it was gone. She must have dropped it.

She heard running footsteps and a young man of about sixteen or seventeen came running up. He saw the problem, pulled a handkerchief from his pocket, and wrapped it around the girl's hand.

"Are you all right, Miss?" he asked Caroline. "You look like you've had a bit of a shock."

"Yes, thank you." Caroline said, pressing the crying Cathy to her. "There, there, we'll go home now. Billy!" she called to the other child.

"At your service, Miss," the young man raised his cap, and went away.

"Your handkerchief?" Caroline called after him. But he just half-turned and waved. She supposed he would not want it now anyway.

She carried Cathy home where Mrs. Barton dabbed her hand with a tincture and re-bandaged it. The little girl was given a raspberry mint.

Caroline wondered who the young man was. She had not seen him before. He was a handsome boy!

ROMANCE

T he next time she went to the Park, she
found herself thinking about and keeping
an eye out for the young man who had
given her his handkerchief for Cathy. The little girl
had fully recovered, and the accident had done
nothing to deter her from her favourite activity. She
and Billy ran up the hillock several times and rolled
down, shrieking in happiness. Caroline kept them to
one part of the hillock only and had made sure there
was nothing harmful that they could hurt
themselves on.

As she lingered at the bottom, she saw the boy stroll
along a path nearby. He was with a girl about ten
years old, his sister, most likely. They approached.
Caroline felt her heart flutter a little. Would he see
her? Would he stop? Should she turn around to greet

him first? But then he'd know she had seen from afar! While feverishly debating the best thing to do, she heard a chummy "Hallo there!" behind her, and she turned around.

"Good morning," she said, being a little more formal than he. He bowed slightly.

"Excuse my forward manner, but I wish to know how the little girl is going on," he said.

"Oh, there she is. As you see, she'sfully recovered!" Caroline indicated the small figure in billowing pinafore at the top of the hillock, screaming with delight at the prospect of another roll.

"I am happy indeed. If I may be so bold as to introduce myself, I am Horace Watts, and may I present my sister, Amelia?"

The girl bowed her head slightly. Olivia recognised her as somebody she had often seen in the park with a woman who was probably her governess. She looked a little out of humour.

"I'm happy to meet you," Caro said. "I am Caroline Davey from the Parsonage."

"Oh, you're the girl who came to live with the Bartons!" exclaimed Amelia, brightening up a little.

"I once had a doll named Amelia," said Caroline. "It was one of my favourite names."

They exchanged their dolls' names with interest. Horace left them and caught Billy up as he came to the bottom of the slope. He trundled him under his arm like a roll of carpet, ran about with him, and came back up to them. Caroline thought this was forward, but Billy thought it was terrific fun, even though Horace was a stranger to him.

"Do you walk here often?" asked Horace, setting the boy down on his feet. "Amelia's governess is on holiday, so I got the order of walking her about the park, though I can't say I'm sorry now, because I've met you."

Another example of his forwardness, and Caroline blushed.

"He didn't want to be seen with me at all," pouted Amelia. "Mother had to make him."

"My friends would laugh at me, Ammy, if they saw me. I'd get no end of ribbing."

"Will you walk with us?" asked Amelia plaintively of Caroline. "My brother won't talk to me about anything as we walk along."

"Oh! Well, all right." She gathered the children and they walked on, the little ones skipping ahead. After a few minutes they came to the gates.

"Will we see you here tomorrow?" asked Amelia. "Please say yes. I don't mind walking with Horace if we will meet you."

"Tomorrow, then," she said, stealing a look at Horace before she took her leave. He was so handsome with a manly face, keen eyes, and strong features. She had never seen a boy like him before.

CLANDESTINE MEETINGS

aroline read the note quickly and hid it before Auntie Mary came into the room. She knew well that her aunt would think that fifteen was far too young to be in love. But she was in love with Horace, and he with her. It had been so for a full year now.

Tell her, Caro, said a little voice.

'No, because she would forbid it.'

'You're deceiving your aunt who has been so good to you.'

'But I'm not doing anything wrong or immoral!'

'Leaving the house when she thinks you are in bed, is wrong.'

She was tired of this conversation between her and her conscience. It wore her down sometimes. The note was a proposition to meet her tonight in their usual place, the old oak tree outside the cemetery.

'I will put an end to this tonight,' she resolved.

"You seem a little distracted," remarked Auntie Mary, coming into the room with an armful of linen. "Is everything all right?"

"Oh yes, Aunt. I was just thinking of how pretty the garden looks in summertime. Those marigolds remind me of Mama. She loved them."

"Your dear Mama. Always a good sister to me."

"Shall I help you with those sheets?"

"Can you patch? No? I will teach you then. Here's an old sheet we'll take the patches from, and here's…" Her aunt spread out the sheets on the table, pointing at this one and that, while Caroline's mind drifted again. Tonight, she would end the trysts with Horace, and tonight, she *would* prevail.

It was easy to slip out unseen. She pretended to go to bed, but after Uncle and Aunt had gone to their room she opened her door very quietly and slipped down the back stairs. The servants had long gone to their attics, and they did not keep a butler or a housekeeper who might prowl about later into the night, checking this and fixing that. Cook was the only servant sleeping downstairs and pausing at her door to hear her snore, Caroline continued down and into the back hall. Her uncle would lock the back door later, but he never bolted it and she took the spare key.

Horace was waiting for her, as usual, by the oak tree. He kissed her and they went along a pathway that led to a quiet leafy road where they were not known. They strolled along.

Horace was a talker, and he talked mostly of himself, so she heard of his news since they had last met. He was to go up to Oxford next year. His father was insisting upon it, and he had heard it was rather a lark, so he was not going to object.

"But I'll miss you, Caro," he said, pausing to twine a little curl she wore on her forehead.

"Horace, I've been thinking -"

"But I will be back for holidays."

"My conscience is bothering me."

"I'll write to you, and you will write to me."

"I can't deceive my Aunt and Uncle any longer."

"What? You're going to tell them about us?"

"No, I'm going to stop coming out at night like this."

"But if you don't come out at night, how are we supposed to meet? Come on, Caro, we have talked of this many times over. We always come to the same conclusion. My family are not acquainted with your family, so there are no social calls between our homes, no luncheons, dinners or picnics. So there is not another way."

"I don't know what the answer is, Horace, but I can't go on deceiving my aunt. I must either tell her, and ask leave to walk out with you, or stop."

"Your aunt is so old-fashioned and a prig. She will not give you leave."

"She is not old-fashioned. She's very modern, and it's not right to deceive her."

"And you're the Rector's niece, and you're afraid you'll be seen and it will be very bad for him."

"That is a consideration, yes."

"But I must see you, Caroline. I must talk with you. I need you. I wish we could elope."

"Oh no, not that, never!" Caroline exclaimed. "And I know you don't mean that anyway."

"No, I don't. But you see how much I love you? Do you not love me?"

"Yes, I do."

"Then say you will continue to see me, Caro."

She sighed. Sometimes she wondered if he did really love her, for he disregarded her feelings on this matter so important to her. It cast her spirits down sometimes.

"I have to go home now," she said. They turned around and set off in the direction of the Parsonage.

"But you will come? Next time I leave a note in the alcove?"

"I will think on it," she said. She did not want another argument. She was tired of arguing with him. She could not win; he always prevailed.

"Goodnight, Caroline." He kissed her when they came to the oak tree. She then crept along by the churchyard, using the wall for cover, until she came to the parsonage. She opened the back door with ease, locked it again and slipped upstairs very quietly. She was in bed and asleep in ten minutes.

SURREY GARDENS

"I'm proposing an outing to Surrey Gardens for you, me, and the older children," said Mr. Barton one evening. "They are showing a reenactment of the Fire of 1666."

"The Fire of London!" cried Percy, "How will they accomplish such a thing, Uncle?"

"That is what we plan to find out," grinned Mr. Barton. "The sets are spectacular, and many things can be done to great effect with the new machinery and inventions we have nowadays."

"Perhaps they use fireworks," Caroline said.

"If we go early, we can walk about first," Mrs. Barton said. "There are exotic plants and flowers from foreign parts, and fountains and bowers. I'll ask Molly to sit up with the little ones."

"It is settled then! Though I have to warn you, it will be nothing like the Great Exhibition of last year."

"But I'm sure that Surrey Gardens has its own charms, dear," said his wife. "There was too much to see in the Great Exhibition, and the crowds made it very uncomfortable. We shall be more leisurely this time."

They set off by omnibus on a sunny August mid-afternoon. Caroline was wearing an emerald gown she had made herself, with an embroidered sash and matching bonnet trimmed with white ribbon. She draped a white lace shawl over her shoulders.

There was a carnival atmosphere as they entered the wide, imposing gates, and in the distance, they heard a lion roar.

Caroline thought that the grounds were heavenly. It was greatly crowded on this fine day, and though it was impossible to see everything the Pleasure Gardens could offer, they walked about admiring the many beautiful and artfully designed gardens, while a band played marches and happy tunes in an elegant pavilion. They grew hungry around six o'clock and partook of a good tea in one of the eating-houses.

As darkness fell, they made their way to the amphitheatre to see the show. Everybody knew the story of the careless baker in Pudding Lane and the dithering Mayor who did not order fire breaks until too late. The sets were so realistic that many cried out and shrank back as the flames rose on the stage, causing showers of sparks to fly in all directions. The Daveys had never seen such a spectacle, and they were enthralled.

"I shall never look at my oven in quite the same way again," declared Mrs. Barton as they surged out with the crowd when it was finished. "Though things were primitive back then, carelessness can cause a fire today as much as almost two hindered years ago. I shall have to tell Cook to be very careful!"

Percy wished to see the animals, but it was too late, and the Gardens were about to close. They walked toward the entrance once more.

As they did so, they decided to wait a little while to allow the greater part of the crowd to exit. Darkness had fallen like a shroud, but the August moon was bright and yellow in the sky.

They strolled on in a leisurely fashion, Mrs. Barton arm-in-arm with her husband, and Caroline and Percy following behind them at a little distance.

On their way in, Caroline had seen a peculiar statue in a grotto up a little side-path, but they had not taken that direction, so she had not seen it close. She mentioned it to her brother, and he agreed that he would divert with her to see it. It would only take a few minutes. But he was hailed suddenly by a schoolfriend, a boy unknown to Caroline, who hastened over to speak to him with animation of the Tableau they had just witnessed. Caroline stood for a moment.

She had not been introduced to the boy, so it was not unmannerly of her to leave her brother and him to their conversation. She slipped away and ran up the path. It was deserted. Nearly everybody had left.

The statue was a disappointment. It was just a piece of carved stone in human form with an ugly face, a gargoyle. She turned to return to her brother but stopped short. A man had slipped out from the trees bordering the path, blocking her way and staring at her. He was a mere six feet away. Caroline instantly became uneasy. She shrank back a little, and he advanced. In the meantime, her brother and friend had walked on a bit and were now out of sight. She darted into the trees, and made her way as quietly as possible through them until a few minutes later she found another path. She branched off to yet another, a larger one, hoping that it would lead her to where she wished to go.

But the main thoroughfare did not materialise.

She was lost. Perhaps she should call out. But if the man was anywhere about, she would give away her location. Then she heard her name being called. She had been missed. She dared not raise her voice but decided to walk in the direction of the shouts.

But the shouts became fainter instead of louder. But there, visible in the moonlight, was a fence, and a street behind it. She climbed over it. At least she was out of the Gardens! Now to find the main entrance and her party, who would be very worried by now. If she followed the fence around, she would eventually find it.

LOST

Caroline was only a little alarmed at first. It seemed to her that if she followed the perimeter of the fence, she would come to the main entrance soon. She hoped that the man was not following her. She glanced behind her. What a relief! He was nowhere to be seen. Which way was the main entrance? There was nobody around to ask!

After walking for about five minutes, she wondered if she was going in the right direction. How big was this park, if she had to walk all the way around it? For the first time, she experienced a suspicion that she could become very lost and might not get home until the morning.

She kept walking, although the Gardens seemed to be behind her now. She had not noticed where she had parted from it, only that a row of small dilapidated houses seemed to replace the fence, and that the fence never reappeared, for at the end of the street, there was another.

It was very late; the moon had retreated behind clouds. It was very dark and she did not know where she was. The houses were shuttered, and only men and a few women were out. Some people looked at her curiously. She wanted to stop and ask them for directions but was afraid. This area was clearly not a respectable one. There was a tavern, and the smell of ale, and somebody was being sick behind a barrel. She walked faster. A man hailed her, tried to stop her, leered at her. The lighting was so poor, she could not make out street signs. She went around a corner, then another, and another. Her heart was hammering now in her chest, and she began to panic. She was lost in a bad area of London at night.

As she walked along, she came upon an open door, and the figure of a woman was in the hallway. She held a candle. A woman would help her. Caroline stopped at the door.

COME INTO MY PARLOUR

"**E**xcuse me," she said, approaching the woman, who advanced out toward the door with her light.

"What is it?" she asked. She was middle-aged, with a white mob-cap and a black shawl.

"I wonder if you could help me. I'm lost." Caroline said.

The woman did not respond immediately.

"Please," said Caroline, desperation in her voice. "I need to find my way home."

The woman shone the candle close to Caroline's face.

"Home, where is home?"

"Cheapside."

"Come in for a minute, dear."

Caroline hesitated only a moment before stepping inside.

"Now come into the parlour, love, and tell me all."

The woman led the way into a small, simply furnished room. There were a few small glass bottles on the table which she took and put into a cupboard.

"Sit down a minute. You look wore out."

Caroline sat gratefully upon the chintz sofa.

"Now, tell me how you come to be lost."

Caroline told her of her evening, about the man following her. It felt good to be in a house away from those bad streets. All was calm here.

"And you live in Cheapside, do you? With your mother and father?"

"No, I'm an orphan. I live with my aunt."

"She must've been good, to take you in. She married?"

"Yes."

"She has children?"

"Yes, three lovely little ones."

"I knows Cheapside. What part?"

"The Parsonage at St. Saviours."

"Oh, I knows it well! I do! I was there a few years ago, I sewed for a lady there, so nice she was There was a young family, oh, if I could but remember her name!"

"Barton!" said Caroline eagerly. "Was it Barton?"

"Barton! That's what it was! My old head! Oh, a lovely lady she was! And is she well?"

"She is very well, but she'll be out of her mind with worry about me by now. I could go home in a cab, if I knew where to find one."

The woman cackled. "Oh dear, no cabs come down this far! No, this is a dangerous place, not even the police come down 'ere. Lucky for you I was at the door, isn't it? Now I 'ave a plan. Stop the night here. I 'have a loverly room upstairs, and tomorrow first thing, we'll go, you and I, to Cheapside, for I would like to see you home safely myself and call upon Mrs. Barton."

Caroline considered the plan. "I don't know. Are you sure there's no possibility of my reaching home tonight? Or even of getting a message to them?"

"No, dear, not that I can think of. Stay the night here, and tomorrow morning, they will be ever so happy to see you returned to them safe and well."

"All right," Caroline said but with reluctance. "That is very good of you," she added.

"That's the right thing ter do. Now I must lock up," said the woman. "My servant is gone fer the night so I shall see you upstairs. What about a nice drink? A drink of milk perhaps?"

After all her walking, Caroline was thirsty.

"It's too much trouble."

"Not at all. Follow me." The woman took the candle and Caroline got up and followed her up a rickety staircase. She felt a little uneasy but banished the feeling away. She threw open a door at the top of the stairs.

"Now, make yourself comfortable. I'll get you one of my daughter's nightgowns. Clean and fresh and ironed."

"Thank you so much. It's so good of you," Caroline said. "May I know your name, please?"

"Oh of course! Anabelle Tait. Mrs. Anabelle Tait. Now get yourself into that nightgown, and hop into bed, and I'll bring in the milk."

Caroline looked about the room. It was furnished with a bed and washstand. The bed had no curtains except for a frilly red swag draped over the bedpost. It was vulgar, but this was a low area. The sheets smelled of body odours, but she tried not to notice.

A few minutes later. the door opened and Mrs. Tait stood by her bed with the milk. There was an odd taste from it, but perhaps the milk in these parts was different. Mrs. Tait waited. Caroline did not want all of it, but she did not wish to be impolite or ungrateful, so she drank it down.

"Goodnight, then," Mrs. Tait said to her. "Sleep well, Miss."

"Goodnight, Mrs. Tait, and thank you again."

Caro settled down and fell instantly asleep.

She had the dream again, the dream that she had had in Fernleigh Manor of being held down by evil shapes. Curses uttered in her ear, but there was no screaming, for there was a hand over her mouth. But she did not awaken this time until morning.

She remembered the dream immediately and shivered. The trauma of becoming lost must have triggered it. She moved her arm, and found that it hurt. The room was just bright enough so that she could see. There was a bruise on her upper arm. How did that get there?

She moved, and became aware that her other arm hurt too. And her face. What had happened? Had she sleepwalked? She had heard of people who walked in their sleep and injured themselves.

As consciousness dawned, she knew something far worse had happened. She hurt all over, carried bruises on numerous parts of her body, and she had been violated in the worst way possible.

Suddenly, she was terrified.

"Mrs. Tait!" she called out. "Mrs. Tait!" She had to summon her urgently to tell her what had happened to her in this house and beg to be taken home immediately.

A few moments later the door opened and a thin woman in servant's garb entered, a jug in her hand.

"Here," she said, pouring the water into the bowl. "This is the only time I'm bringing water to you. From now on you can get it yourself."

"I'm leaving here today!" cried Caroline. "Now, this minute! Send Mrs. Tait to me!"

The girl shook her head, laughed, and went out.

Caroline sat up, but her clothes were not where she had left them, neatly filed on the chair. There was no wardrobe.

Her clothes were missing.

EVIL LIVES HERE

The room Caroline was in faced a high brick wall. Without clothes, she could not go anywhere, not even downstairs. She could hear a man's voice so she could not even go down with the sheet wrapped about her. She lay in bed, aching all over, shaking with cold and distress, her mind in shock. Mrs. Tait did not come.

At last the door opened and the woman she wanted to see entered. She had a bundle of clothes in her arms.

"Get up now. Get dressed."

"Mrs. Tait, I have been waiting for you to come for some time. My family will be frantic with worry, and what's worse, I have met with a brutal assault here in this house! I have been ruined! And somebody took my clothes!"

"These are your clothes now. Get up. There's work to be done."

"Work? I'm going home!"

Mrs. Tait was silent. Caroline stared at her in dawning horror. *Was this the same woman who had sheltered her last night?*

The milk! The milk had been drugged!

She was staring evil in the face in Mrs. Tait.

"You *know*," she said. "You took advantage! Did you send my tormentor to me? Who was he? I shall go to the police directly!"

"Police? I have a friend in the police. He comes 'ere often. He came here last night. Anytime anybody makes a complaint to the police, he makes sure it gets torn up."

"You said you would help me! I trusted you!"

She merely smiled.

"You can't intend to keep me here! For how long?"

"You can't leave, even if I allowed you to walk out the door. Where would you go? You're ruined, you said it yourself. Ruined for life. Your uncle is a churchman. They wouldn't want you back now. You would ruin *them*. You are different to what you were yesterday. You can't ever go back to yesterday and being respectable. You're only good for one thing now. Get up, get dressed, the scullery needs scrubbin' out. Look sharp. You'll get nothing to eat until you've done some work."

"Mrs. Tait!" The plea was in a horrified whisper to the women's back as she went out the door.

The clothes were drab, and they smelled. They were the clothes of a lower servant. She dressed with copious weeping and went downstairs, only to be handed a bucket and a scrubbing brush. After that, she had to sweep the backyard, and wash linens in cold water and hang them out on a clothesline. She hurt all over. She wept all that day and refused to eat the stale roll thrust at her later by the servant Annie, who looked down on her as if she were a piece of dirt.

When evening came, she had made a plan to escape. When nobody was looking, she stole toward the front door, but was met there by a large growling dog who was lying in front of it. He got up, showed his fangs, and drooled. A man with scars on his face came out of the parlour door, the room she had been shown into and made welcome the night before. Was it only last night? He was the ugliest man she had ever seen, his face scarred, his chin stubbled, his appearance unkempt, greasy, and odious. He did not need to utter a word. She shrank back to the scullery. The back door led to the backyard, which was full of scrap metals, old mattresses, and all kinds of junk. High walls enclosed it. There was no way out.

NO ESCAPE

I t had been three weeks, and Caroline felt that she had died and gone to Hell. Every day and every night was the same. She had lost weight, and she had even lost her name, for Mrs. Tait told her that Caroline was unsuitable. She was to be Lilya from now on. *Luvly Lilya*, said Mrs. Tait, with a laugh.

Her mind was constantly on her home. What were they doing now? Was her aunt in tears every day? Did the children ask for her? Did Percy blame himself? What did Horace think? She longed to be with him now, but Horace would never look at her again, even if she did escape this place. She was fifteen years old and her life was finished.

She missed Horace! She was sure that if he knew where she was, he would come and rescue her.

And where was God? He was absent too! He didn't come here, to this place. She supposed that it was too evil for Him to be here. If she prayed, would He hear her? Or was He angry with her, for sneaking out at night to see Horace, and had left her to her own devices?

She remembered the presence of Love when she had been in Fernleigh Manor. It was absent now. She had been abandoned! Where was God? Why did He not get her away from this place?

Were her family looking for her?

Mrs. Tait seemed to guess her thoughts. She frequently said: *"Your people know well what's 'appened, and they will leave well enough alone. It would go very bad for them if you came back. Everybody would know what you were. Some will say you were willing, for there's always people who think that way. There will be gossip and your uncle would not be able to stand the shame. He'd lose his parish. You couldn't be in the same house as anybody's children. It would be a scandal. No, they wouldn't want you back. Anyway, you're not their child, are you?"*

"Stop!" cried Caroline. She saw the woman's lips curl in a cruel smile. She was enjoying herself.

"You were so easy," Mrs. Tait sometimes said, especially in the evenings when she was downing gin from the small bottles she kept everywhere. *"You walked in my door! I didn't have to promise you a situation, or put an advertisement in the paper, or go off to meet you at the station, or convince your family I'd look after you, or anything. You just walked into my parlour! There for the taking."*

Caroline felt a great fury burn in her breast, but she dared not show it. At any sign of *'cheek'* as Mrs. Tait put it, she called for Pilot, the mastiff, who bounded to wherever she was, with his sharp fangs and drooling jaws. When Caroline refused to eat, Pilot was called, and growled until she ate. He seemed to have been trained to intimidate and knew his job. Even the dog considered her worthless.

There was one other way out that she would try. The parlour window looked out on the street. It was a sash window. She would have to plan it when Joe the Bully was not there of course. She was thankful that Joe was not one of the men who came at night. He revolted her more than any of them.

Again, Mrs. Tait seemed to know what she was thinking.

"The cop on his beat will bring you back if you get out. There's no point in escaping; he'd bring you right back. He likes you."

"How long are you going to keep me here for?" asked Caroline, now in despair.

"For some time to come. And by the way, the clients are complaining that you don't seem to be 'aving a nice time. Some ave complained that you weep an' take on. Don't. You make 'em feel *guilty*. So you're to smile and look pleased to see 'em and let on you like 'em, even if you don't. I 'ad to do it when I started."

Caroline looked at her, thinking that perhaps that would be her way out. The men would leave her alone if she was unpleasant to be with, and she'd be useless to this evil woman. But again, Mrs. Tait seemed to guess her thoughts.

"If you don't do as I say I'll *interduce you* to some very nasty people," Mrs. Tait threatened. "You'll wish you 'ad never been born when they're finished with you."

This frightened her enough that she willed herself to obey.

LANYARD LANE

August became September, and the leaves from the few trees that grew in Palm Street (whoever had named it had a warped sense of humour) blew about. By October it was dark, gloomy and the gutters were filling with rain. The tiny backyard swam in dirt and the old mattresses thrown there were sodden through. There was a colony of rats nesting there.

One day in November she was given a cloak and shoes and told to follow Joe. He was to take her to another house.

She became instantly frightened.

"Why?" she asked. The man terrified her.

Over the last weeks, Annie had thawed a little, so she explained.

"There's a bigger 'ouse than this one, that 'er sister runs. This is for the new girls. There's a girl coming on a train today from Yorkshire. She answered her advertisement for a housemaid in a respectable 'ouse, and she will meet her at the station. She gets all dressed up and poses as the housekeeper. She'll hire a hackney and says she must go by Palm Street to see an old servant she looks after. In she comes with the girl, and that's that." she chuckled. Caroline felt disgusted.

"Where is this house I have to move to?" she asked coldly.

"It's in Gullseye. By the Docks. Lots of custom there!" she laughed again.

"Don't even think of trying to give Joe the slip," Mrs. Tait said before she put on her best hat and cloak to go to the station. "He knows where you lived, and you wouldn't want anyfink to happen to your little ncousins, would you?"

Caroline felt so broken by now that even the thought of escape seemed beyond her. She was sure it was useless to try. She felt numbed all the time, frozen in her circumstances, but this new threat to hurt people close to her, helpless children, put away any lingering thought of escape.

Even the prospect of leaving the house frightened her. It should have given her hope. She should be glad to leave it, but it was not that way. She felt terrified of what lay ahead, and found herself wanting to stay, even though she hated it. The unfamiliar was even more feared.

Joe led Pilot on a leash. Caroline walked fearfully beside him. It felt very strange to be out. She could not raise her head. She was sure that everybody knew about her. It was a silly thought, but it was there. They walked toward the docklands. The streets got older and more dilapidated. They turned into a street named Lanyard Lane. They entered the Lanyard Arms. There was an odour of beer and tobacco in this dimly lit room with a dance area in the centre. A woman with fair, curly hair hanging loose around her shoulders come up to them.

"A new one, is it?"

"Aye. This is Lilya." Joe turned on his heel and left.

"I'm Carla. Come in," said the woman. She brought her to the back rooms and introduced her to an older woman, Mrs. McDonald, who resembled Mrs. Tait. Her sister!

The stairway to the rooms above led from the public house, in a dark corner, as if it was supposed to be hiding there. She was taken upstairs.

"This will be where you conduct business," Mrs. McDonald said, throwing open a door to reveal a cramped chamber decorated in yellow and scarlet. It was none too clean, and the wallpaper was old and torn. A cracked mirror hung on the wall. The only other furniture was a chair and a tiny table with a jug and bowl.

She was given two garish gowns, a bonnet, an old hat, a shawl and petticoats, and items like combs, powders, rouge, and tawdry jewellery.

"They're our property," warned Mrs. McDonald holding up the gowns, one of which had a vulgar, low neckline. "And if you try to get away in them, we'll have you arrested for theft. You'll be followed every time you go out for customers. We know all the tricks. Get dressed and put on the rouge."

A girl named Rita, not much older than she, came into her room after Mrs. McDonald had left.

"You'll get used to it, Lilya. If you get no business in the tavern, you have to walk the streets. So look lively downstairs. And like you're having a good old time. That always attracts customers. Gin will help you, if you're not in the mood for frivolity. My real name is Bess, by the way."

A ship had come in and the public house was filled with rowdy foreign sailors. A tinny piano played a waltz. She tried to look happy, but she thought of the poor girl from Yorkshire who by now had walked into the trap in Palm Street.

The world was evil indeed.

"This is our new girl, Luvly Lilya," cried Mrs. McDonald, pulling her into the centre of the dance floor. "Who would like a dance with Luvly Lilya?"

As Caroline danced, trying to look happy, she espied a young man in a corner drinking by himself. He was fair-haired and lean, and had a tired, rather hopeless look about him, staring at what was taking place around him in between sips of ale. One of the other girls approached him, dancing her way along and swinging a feather boa to attract his attention. He finished his drink in one gulp and got up, pretending not to see her, and swept toward the door.

On his way out, he glanced in Caroline's direction, and as she was watching him, their eyes met briefly. She looked away, ashamed. *He is a virtuous man*, she thought. *Like Percy or Uncle Will. He thinks I'm an immoral woman, and I am.*

"You know that chap?" asked the sailor, wheeling her around in a lively waltz. "Your jilted sweetheart, is it?"

"Oh no, I don't know him." Caroline flashed a smile at the sailor, because Mrs. McDonald had come from the back, and was watching her to see if she was doing her job.

35

ARTHUR

Arthur Ellis walked away from the Lanyard Arms and went to his lodging, a dirty old building where he was charged twopence a night for a flea-ridden mattress and one filthy blanket. The hour in the Lanyard Arms had not done anything to convince him that England was where he belonged.

His day had begun and ended badly.

He had not been picked for work today either at the Docks. He seemed invisible to the quay ganger who called out *"You! And you! And you!"* every morning when the casual labourers surged forward to be taken on for a day.

He wished he'd stayed in Van Demiens Land, or after he had got his Certificate of Freedom, crossed over the Bass Strait to New South Wales. He could have made a life for himself there. Many did. They worked on sheep farms, saved, bought their own land, and were on their way to becoming prosperous farmers, and even leaders in their fledgling communities.

But he had wanted to return to England when his sentence was up, to go back to Nottingham to clear his name. So far, he had not got past London Docklands. How many times when breaking stone in the quarries or herding sheep on the farms had he dreamed of his homecoming? Older men had cautioned him. *It won't be like that, Art. You'll bear the stigma of a convict all your life. You'll never get took on anywhere. Stay here and make somethin' of yourself. Here, there are so many of us, it doesn't seem to matter that we were sent out in disgrace from England, rebels and rioters and robbers an' all sorts.*

But it ate him up inside that he had been convicted of a crime he had not committed and that his family had suffered shame because of it. There had also been the nagging resentment that, though he had grown to like many of the other convicts, he was not one of them. Most were men who were familiar with the inside of jail cells, who had not given up their lives of crime despite the threats of imprisonment. His background had been very different.

Arthur was the son of a clergyman, and he had been preparing to go to Oxford with a view to taking Orders as soon as he turned twenty-four, becoming curate to his father in Nottinghamshire, and taking over the living when he retired. He could never become a clergyman now.

But now he wished he had listened to the older men. England was no place for a man who had a stain on his character. And there was a hopeless sort of misery here, ragged masses of humanity and the foulest air. He had become used to wide open spaces.

He hadn't money for transport, but he could walk home doing odd jobs on the way. He was well-used to hardship and hunger. A man who worked on a chain gang building roads could set himself to anything.

The Lanyard Arms was one of the seediest places he had ever been in, and that was saying something after the run-down shacks he had seen in Hobart. He had gone there for a glass of ale and it was soon obvious that the place was a brothel. But that girl, dragged out on the floor and paraded like a cow or a sheep at the Mart. He had watched her as she took the floor, and he thought there was something different about her in comparison to the others. The other women had a hard, seasoned look, like the woman who had come toward him waving the feather boa. This other girl was young, and not used to a dance floor, though she was making a good effort to be acquainted with it. She was not at home in the Lanyard Arms. Something in her demeanour was lacking. She did not wear her immodest gown well. He knew a forced smile, a pretense at levity. He'd become a good reader of hearts. Their eyes had met briefly, and she had looked away in shame.

Poor girl, whoever she was.

All that evening, Arthur could not get the girl out of his mind. He went to sleep thinking of her, and awoke remembering her pretty face, sad eyes, and false smile. He sat up on his mattress, frowning. There was something amiss. He had no inclination now to travel north until he had found out more.

Therefore, he looked for work that day, and was lucky. The ganger's finger pointed at him, "You!" Was it really he who had been called? As soon as he realised it was he, he bounded forward. He unloaded a ship carrying casks of beer, textiles, and other goods, and at the end of the day had a sixpence jingling in his pocket added to the few pennies already there.

He bought a pie from a stall, and having eaten, he made his way to the Lanyard. He was early, by design. He had no intention of allowing her to be swept off by a rival for her attentions. She was not down yet.; He ordered a drink and took it to a table not far from the stairs.

He was approached by the older woman, obviously the Madam, or the Bawd, which description fitted her best.

"Ah, you are back, sir. You left in a hurry last night, I wondered that you saw nothing that pleased you?"

"I had an appointment last night. But I did see a girl I liked, so if I could have her company when she comes down, I'd be much obliged."

"Which girl?"

"Her name is Lilya."

"Luvly Lilya! She only arrived yesterday, and already she's a favourite! Ah, here she is. Lilya, you are to spend time with this gent, here."

Arthur got to his feet and bowed his head. Mrs. McDonald looked at him curiously, smirked, and left.

She wore a different gown than last night. This one was red with black lace, and again, she did not look comfortable in it. She had rouge on her cheeks and carmine on her lips. Her eyes were downcast but as if remembering, she looked up suddenly and smiled. A false smile.

"It's all right," he said quietly after a short pause. "You don't have to smile with me."

The smile faded, to be replaced with a bewildered expression.

"I want to introduce myself. I'm Arthur Ellis." He spoke rather slowly, which Caroline interpreted as a kind of sincerity in his character. His blue-grey eyes seemed gentle, though his face was brown and weather-beaten, and he had an old scar on his cheek. His hands were calloused, those of a working man.

"Mr. Ellis, I'm obliged."

"Sit down and join me in a drink." He called for the barman, and she said she wanted gin. He ordered it for her, feeling that she was too young for such a strong drink, but she was following orders, perhaps. There had been places like this in Hobart, and the convict girls, when finished their sentences, often found themselves induced to work there.

"Lilya, what's your real name?" He kept his tone low.

"That's my name," she said a little suspiciously.

"No, it's not. I don't know anybody in England with the name Lilya. I bet you're Anna or Lucy."

Why did she look frightened?

The other girls had come down. The place was beginning to fill up and the piano had begun a tinny waltz.

"Don't you want to dance?" she asked him.

"No, I want to talk with you, privately. *Only* talk."

Her large dark eyes were curious.

"*Why?*" She sounded amazed.

"You don't belong here, I know," he said then.

"How do you know?" asked Caroline, fidgeting. She flashed a smile again.

"If you don't mind my asking you, how old are you?"

"Eighteen."

He shook his head. Caroline looked uneasily at the next table. A few of the girls were sitting there, drinking, chatting, and waiting for men. She could not say anything, but it occurred to her that this man was different to the others.

"Only talk?" she asked again, quite surprised.

He nodded.

"Follow me," she said, as she led the way upstairs.

TALK

They entered her room. She looked a little uncertain. Arthur sat down in the only chair and she sat demurely on the bed. She took a little shawl, a fichu, from the bedstead and wrapped it over her bosom.

"What do you want to talk about?" she asked. "You'll have to pay for my time no matter what, you know," she added hurriedly.

"That's all right. I want to talk about you."

Caroline looked down and folded her hands. She did not know what to think. Finally she raised her head.

"Did my uncle and aunt send you?" she asked in a hopeful tone.

He shook his head.

"Why should they? Did you run away from them?"

She stood up suddenly.

"You're the police! They will kill me!"

He raised his hand in a gesture of protest. Again, he took his time replying.

"No, no. Do I look like the police? I've just returned from a sentence in Van Diemens Land, sent there for seven years for a crime I did not commit."

"Is it so, really?" She digested this, searching his face. "When did you get back?"

"Not a week ago. I came in here last night for a drink, and saw you. I was curious. Why did you ask if your uncle and aunt sent me?"

"I didn't run away," she said guardedly. "I was lost, and this is where I ended up." She gazed at him intently. "You don't look surprised!"

"I've seen the worst in human nature," he said. "The very worst. Nothing surprises me."

She gazed at him again. She seemed to be pondering something.

"I wager you never heard of this, though," she said. "There was this girl, fifteen years old, from a very respectable family, who went to Surrey Gardens one day with her aunt and uncle and brother."

He listened intently as Lilya spoke of this unfortunate girl. When she came to the part when she woke in the morning, she dissolved into tears and could not go on, but buried her head in her hands, sobbing quietly.

He could not move to her, to pat her head or her shoulder to comfort her, as she could misunderstand and think he was like the other men.

Instead, he leaned forward in this chair.

"May I know more about your poor friend Caroline?"

She glanced at him. Her face was red with weeping.

"And you see Caroline Davey here," she said. "Trapped here now."

"Not trapped, Miss Davey. You must not think like that. You must always have hope."

"No, I cannot. I will never go home again. I know that." Her head turned towards the window. "It's impossible," she said bitterly. "I can't go back to what I was. Did you ever hear of such an evil thing to happen anybody?"

He had a fleeting memory, which he tried to put away. The hulk of a man, his mate in the cell at Hempley, shortly after his arrest.

"I must go," he said. "Who do I pay?"

She held out her hand and he put sixpence into it.

"Will that be enough?"

"Yes. I have to go downstairs again now. Thank you. You are a gentleman, I see. I mean that in the sense of you being a good, gentle man. Because there are a few gentlemen I met in the other house, who are not good or decent at all. They delight in engaging in low activities, and their families never know that they are the most disgusting creatures. Can you believe that?"

"I can believe it very well," he said heartily, with a wry smile. Her remark about his being a gentle man amused him, for he was also of that rank of men known as gentlemen, but he had lost all trace of that.

He nodded. They went down again together.

"I have to go away tomorrow, but when I come back, I'd like to see you," he said. "For more talk,' he added.

"You know where to find me," she said in a monotonous tone.

He left.

"What an admirer you've got there," Mrs. McDonald said to her, her hand out. "Hand it over, Lilya."

Caroline did as bidden. Her earnings belonged to Mrs. McDonald.

"Sixpence! I will let you have a penny out of it. Here," Mrs. McDonald put a coin into her hand.

She sat at a table and hoped not to be approached by anybody for a time. She felt touched in her heart. Mr. Ellis was a decent man, the kind of person that did not belong in this rotten place, a kind-hearted man. He had made her feel almost human, almost like a person again.

38

MIDDLEDENE

Arthur left London the following morning. He had again awakened to the thought of Caroline Davey, and he pondered if he should postpone his journey north. But he had urgent business, business that he had thought about for seven years and more.

He had little doubt that Miss Davey was telling the truth. He wondered briefly if he should report it to the police, but it was too complicated at present, and might endanger her.

It was a long trudge from London to Middledene in Nottinghamshire, but in a few days, tired and footsore, grateful for any rides he got from passing farmers who wanted to talk to a stranger or just do a good turn, Arthur at last saw the bell tower of the church he knew so well, St. Nicholas. It rose above the treetops to greet him, or was it to mock him? It should have been his parish. Who had the living now, and more importantly, what had happened to his family? He had had no news in seven long years.

As he drew closer to Middledene, coming over the hill that afforded a good view of the village and its environs, familiar sights caused memories to flood him. There was the old gate to Norris field, still on one hinge and half-falling off. There was the Fenwick cottage, methodically and flawlessly thatched. They were still living there then, as the Fenwicks were the best thatchers for thirty miles. There were children playing in the Daisy Field, just as he had done. He looked over a hedge to see them, seeing himself and his playmates. They would not know him. What's this? Two new houses! Middledene had moved on after the events of 1846.

He heard the sound of forging before he came to the blacksmith's. It stood as it always had, a long, low building of cut stone, the doorway in the shape of a horseshoe, and as always, open summer and winter. It was just across from the Middledene Inn and its stables. Mr. Leamy was blacksmith no more, of course. He had probably never recovered from the blow. He had been almost sixty when it happened.

The new smithy was a young man. Arthur stopped to watch him for a moment, his mind returning him to that time, his memories blazing to life like the fire in the forge. He could almost hear again the laughter and banter with Matthew Harries, the younger son of the Squire and his best friend, as they tramped the rugged roads, leaped over stiles and ditches, and waded in the streams. Neither had a care in the world.

39

HAPPIER DAYS

In 1670, the first Mr. Harries in the district reaped the reward of a wise investment in the West Indies, bought a great deal of land near the Lake District, and built a fine house in the area of Middledene. There had been no village near the spot chosen for his home, so he set about establishing one to serve the needs, physical and spiritual, of his grand residence. He called it Middledene, after the name chosen for his home. Within twenty years, the village was well-established, and it boasted every trade and amenity needed by that time. He was a good landlord, and Middledene prospered. His son and subsequent heirs were equally good.

The church was in the same style of the mansion, red sandstone. To serve the needs of his household, the first Mr. Harries bestowed the living upon a Mr. Ellis. The living had passed from father to son in every generation since, and the two families were always on good terms, visited each other, and dined in each other's homes.

The summer of 1846 was a pleasant one in Middledene. Arthur Ellis and Matthew Harries were the same age, but went to different boarding schools, and summer saw them happily reunited and full of schemes. This summer, however, Mr. Ellis had some different plans for his son. He was a rather serious man, but very affectionate towards his family.

"This entire summer is not to be spent haring about the countryside, Arthur. You will be a clergyman like me, and your training will begin young. I'm not simply a clergyman on Sundays, as you know. There is a great deal more to serving God. We serve his people. You must be trained in the habit of serving others."

"Yes, sir," said Arthur meekly, if a little glumly. Matthew had written that he had new fishing tackle, and he was eager to try it out.

"I'm going to engage you in certain tasks to be accomplished daily before you skedaddle off with

Master Matthew. The first one will be visitation of the sick and the elderly, in the mornings, with me."

"Yes, Father." Arthur felt himself becoming more glum.

"Master Arthur will have to have some amusement!" Mrs. Quinn, the cook, was bustling about the dining room. She did not usually come up there but she was training a new maid. She tended to be outspoken, but the rector and his wife did not mind. She loved Arthur.

"Do not be uneasy on Arthur's account, Mrs. Quinn," said the rector, an indulgent smile on his face. "He is to have plenty of free time. I had a great boyhood, and so will he. In the afternoons, Arthur, you may go about as you please."

Arthur found himself enjoying himself with his father more than he had thought. He knew the cottagers, and the poor people. He knew everybody in Middledene. It was such a small place that everybody knew everybody else. But now he found it rather interesting to visit the needy cottagers with his father, and show concern and caring for not only their spiritual needs, but also for their physical wants. He fixed a loose window sash for Widow Byrne, and chopped wood for the emaciated Mr.

Jenks, who was close on ninety years old, feeling the cold even in June.

"You see, Arthur, we cannot go into a house, read them a Bible verse, and go away satisfied. Who in the Bible wrote that we cannot say *'God bless you, stay warm, eat well'* to a poor person, and then go away without helping them, if they are hungry and shivering with cold?"

"I don't know, Papa!"

"Find it tonight, and you can tell me. Now, it's time to go home. What have you and Master Matthew planned for the rest of the day?"

"We're going fishing down by Farmer Kent's."

"Good, well enjoy yourself, lad. Is Master Gregory accompanying you?"

"No, he has some other scheme. I don't think, Father, he likes to spend time with his younger brother now. Not since he went to Oxford."

"Indeed. I am just as pleased he will be about another scheme."

"Why is that, Father?"

"He has altered. The last time I met him, which was at Easter, he did not speak to me or to your mother with any respect. I formed the opinion that he thought me an old fool."

Arthur considered this.

"He has altered, Father. He's got rather snobbish. I don't like to speak ill of him, but he holds himself very superior to everybody here."

"He is of the first family here," his father reflected. "But while I hesitate to speak ill of him either, I have heard that he has kept bad company in Oxford, and has amassed debts. I tell you this only for you to be on your guard. Should he join you and Matthew, he may be likely to abuse the good Christian values that we hold dear, that I and your mother have taught you. You will see evil enough in the world in your time. Of that I'm certain. But for evil to be presented as a lark, or a joke-"

"What kind of evil, Father?"

"Gambling, avariciousness, drunkenness. That is what I speak of. I'm not saying that Master Gregory has indulged in any of these. But young men away from the confines of home for the first time meet great temptation, even debauchery. But you are too young to know what that is."

"I think I do know, sir," he said as they turned in the gate to the neat parsonage.

"Another matter, Arthur. Try to discourage Eleanor from liking him so much. She does not listen to her mother at all on that point, or to Susanna."

"I am afraid, Father, that she has liked him since they were young."

"He was different then."

Eleanor was nineteen years old. She was a quiet girl who gave the cold shoulder to every man who had shown interest in her. Her parents feared that it was on account of Master Gregory, but she refused to speak of it. Susanna, a year younger, was far more sensible, and was engaged to a gentleman from the large town six miles off, Hempley. He was a Captain in the 59th Regiment of Foot which was presently in Malta, and *billets-doux* sailed over and back with regularity. They were to be married on his next home leave.

"Here you are at last!" she cried. "We thought you'd gotten lost. And we're ready to begin luncheon. Mama didn't know where you were, did you, Mama?"

They went eagerly to the dining room and seated themselves at the table. Their new maid, Lucy Little, served them. Arthur often found himself looking at her. She was about his own age, and uncommonly pretty, with dark curls, delicate features and wide eyes.

"How was poor Mr. Jenks?" asked Mrs. Ellis, drawing his attention away from the girl. She had employed Lucy with a little reluctance, but her mother had been laundress for the parsonage for many years. Her son was at a dangerous age for falling in love with just the wrong girl.

MASTER GREGORY

Matthew and Arthur had a fine afternoon by the stream. Showers threatened but held off, and the day was just cloudy enough for the fish to swim out from cover.

Arthur was curious now about Master Gregory.

"What is he up to this afternoon?"

"Oh, I don't know. He has friends in Hempley. I hope there isn't a big row when he comes back, though."

"Why should there be?"

"Because he and Papa quarrel all the time. I say, if I tell you something, will you promise not to repeat it?"

"I promise."

Matthew hesitated a moment, before he plunged in.

"It's this. He wants more money, and Papa won't give it to him. He says that all of his friends at Oxford have more than he. Some have their own gigs and teams to drive them. They are all going to the seaside for August. My father says that their parents must be fools to allow them all that at their age, and he is not giving him the money to go. It's very unpleasant to have to go on listening to them like that. I wish he would go away. I heard him beg my mother for money also. She said no, too. He called them mean-spirited and said awful things. I say, Arthur, you won't repeat any of this to anybody, will you? I mean, to your father and mother?"

"No, of course not."

"Promise?"

"I promise."

Though they had been lifelong friends, Arthur was at times conscious of the difference in rank between the Harries and everybody else in the village. They were high gentry. The Ellis' family was low gentry. It was a demonstration of great trust that Matthew confided the troubles of his family to him. He may have regretted it already. The very rich do not confide in their inferiors. They kept their affairs to themselves, and were trained to do so from a young age.

"You see, there's something else." Matthew hesitated. "He took something of Mother's. Some jewellery. I saw him with it. He did not see me. I saw him leave her room, stuffing it into his pocket."

"Has she missed it yet?"

"No, not yet. It might be something she doesn't look at, so she might never miss it. I hope she never misses it, because her maid would be suspect, and she's nice."

"My brother is a thief," he said then. "Promise me you will never tell a soul?"

"I promise."

Matthew cheered up as they got a bite and they reeled in a trout, and then another. As they ambled along the village street on their way home, a horseman caught up with them and slowed his mount to keep pace.

"I say, you have had a successful time!" said Master Gregory. "Is the parsonage to have trout for dinner, then?"

"I hardly think so. Mother has dinner ordered, and in any case I want to give mine to Mr. Leamy. He likes trout."

"Oh, that old miser. You should sell it to him, make him take out one of his carefully-hidden gold coins."

"Why do you think Mr. Leamy has money, Greg? He's only a blacksmith," remarked Matthew.

"He has money because he never got married, never spends it, and saves it all. He's well-known to have a fortune. I wonder where the old fellow hides it."

They reached the blacksmith's. Mr. Leamy was not there. He was probably in his house at the back. They went around there and found him sitting inside sewing a patch on an old shirt.

The house was a shambles. Serving girls came and went, unable to bear the restrictions of the old man, expected to clean without moving anything or touching various objects. He was a quarrelsome fellow and was only happy on his own. The landlady at the inn sent his dinner over every day, and he fended for himself for breakfast and supper.

"A trout, eh? Thank ye, lads. I'll give it to Mrs. Timmons to cook for me." The four people filled the one-roomed cabin.

Master Gregory's eyes darted about everywhere.

"I say, you should have a better place than this after all your work down through the years, old man."

Mr. Leamy raised himself up with dignity.

"I'm fine as I am, thank you, Master Harries."

"Oh, as you wish, of course. But my father owns this cabin, and he wouldn't like to see it run-down. He wants all his tenants to look after their homes."

"He has never complained to me," Mr. Leamy said with testiness.

"Oh, of course not." The young man stepped about the room.

"There's a loose floorboard here," he said. "And here. Not safe, is it?"

"It's quite safe enough, thank you," Mr. Leamy said stiffly, suspiciously. "I thank thee for the trout, lads." It was a dismissal.

They left and walked up the street in silence, Gregory leading his horse. Arthur felt angry with him.

They reached the Parsonage, and to Arthur's surprise, Gregory tied up his horse to the post outside the gate.

"I haven't seen your parents for a long time. I'd like to pay my respects," he said.

Arthur hoped that he wished to see Eleanor, but this was followed by the thought that he did not want to see his sister married to a thief.

Master Gregory was greeted with courteous warmth by his parents, and as usual with many blushes and a little confusion from Eleanor, to whom he paid no attention beyond a bow. Miss Susanna regarded him with contempt but was all politeness. Mrs. Ellis ordered tea, and then Arthur guessed the real reason for Master Gregory's wish to enter the house.

Lucy brought the tea in, and Gregory could not take his eyes from her. He had heard of the pretty maid at the parsonage, and wished to take a view of her himself.

Arthur felt angry. He was angry at Gregory for feigning interest in paying his respects to his parents, angry at Eleanor, who was so hopelessly and incurably in love with a scoundrel like Gregory, angry with himself for being jealous of Gregory, who caught Lucy's eye in an expression of admiration, and angry at Lucy herself, whose long eyelashes fluttered a little in return.

41
NEWS

The new blacksmith looked up. "What do you want?" he asked roughly, but not unkindly. Arthur realised that he looked like the vagrant he was, scruffy and ragged, his beard wild, his clothes with bits of straw still clinging to them after sleeping in a barn the night before.

"Food," said Arthur, hardly knowing that he was responding with his greatest need at that time. "I've had a long journey."

"Go around to the house at the back. My wife will give you summat." He returned to his work.

The ramshackle house with old, dirty curtains and crooked furniture was no more. In its place was a neat cottage, freshly painted, with shrubs and a vegetable garden.

"Your husband sent me around for a bite to eat," he said to the young woman who was taking clothes from the washing line.

"Wait a minute then."

He sat on an old rock that had been there in Mr. Leamy's time. The young woman appeared with a hunk of bread spread with bacon fat and a large mug of tea.

"Thank you, Ma'am. I was in this village a long time ago, and knew a Mr. Leamy then, who lived here. You've done wonders with this place."

"Oh, thank you."

"What happened to Mr. Leamy?"

"That poor old fellow! He's on the parish, over at Hempley."

"In the workhouse?"

"Yes, poor old fellow, quite mad."

He tore off a piece of bread with his teeth and drank some of the sweetened tea. It felt refreshing and he almost caught himself thanking God for the simple kindness of country folk.

"The family at the Big House, are they still there?"

"Yes, the Harries."

"The older man?"

"That's him. And his wife. They're good landlords, pulled down the rotten old house that was here, and built this nice new cottage for us."

"There were two sons there."

"Yes, I never saw either of them. The older one is off somewhere, as he was a great disappointment to his parents. He's in France or someplace and there he will stay, I suppose, until his father dies, which I hope won't be for a long time, as the son is nothing like the father, from what I hear."

"And the younger son? What did he do?"

"Mr. Matthew is also a dreadful disappointment to his mother and father. He drinks. Nobody seems to know where he is now or how he's living, for I hear that he has no contact with his parents. It's terrible, in't? All the money in the world can't buy happiness, that's what my mother says."

Arthur considered the news about Matthew with some interest.

There was a little silence. The woman continued to take her clothes in from the line, dropping them into a large basket.

Arthur finished the bread and drained the tankard. He felt strengthened straight away. The fat in the sandwich and the invigorating tea had revived him.

"I thank you, Mrs.—?"

"Taylor."

"Mrs. Taylor. You and your husband are good people."

"Don't mention it. Not many strangers come through here. But since Hempley got the railway, there have been more than before. Did you come by train?"

"No, I walked. I walked all the way from London, in fact, just getting rides now and then."

"Oh, that's a long way off. And are you staying here at the village? Do you have a trade, then? You must have a trade of some sort. Are you a tinsmith or a stonemason or summat?"

He smiled to himself. Country people were very curious. A sleepy village would not have much that was new. He guessed that the stranger that had walked from London would cause some talk, and she wanted information on that score, not just for her own satisfaction, but to tell the other women when she went to the pump for water.

"I'm a stonemason," he said, thinking of all the stone he had broken in his days in penal servitude, though none of it involved the delicate craft of engraving or polishing, just the brute force of smashing rock. "And I'm skilled with animals, sheep in particular."

He set the empty plate and tankard on the ground beside him.

"If I might ask you one more question," he said, getting to his feet and clearing his throat. "The Ellis family at the Parsonage, are they still there?"

"Oh no, Mister. Before my husband and I came here, they were gone. The family there now is named Robinson."

"They have gone! Why was that?"

"Some sort of scandal." She picked up her basket of crisp, fresh laundry.

"What kind of scandal?"

"As I've 'eard, the son was accused of stealing and was imprisoned. Actually, it was Mr. Leamy he stole from. Imagine, a clergyman's son, gone so bad! He brought the whole family down with him."

Arthur felt full of despair at this news.

"Do you know of their whereabouts now?"

She shook her head, swinging her basket on her hip.

"No," she looked at him curiously. "Why do you want to know? Were you well acquainted with them?"

"I was. I'm trying to find them."

"I'm sure Mr. Robinson will know where they are." She waited expectantly, reluctant to go into the house until she had seen him away.

"Thank you, Mrs. Taylor." He tipped his cap.

"God go with you," she replied.

God! He wanted nothing more to do with God.

S ure he would not be easily recognised, Arthur continued through the village. It was late afternoon and shadows were lengthening on the cobbled street. It was much as he remembered it. Some people going about their business with the butcher or the greengrocer glanced at the stranger, but he attempted no greeting to anybody, though he thought he recognised more than a few. He looked above the rooftops at the bell tower of St. Nicholas looming nearer and nearer.

He came to the bend in the road around which he knew he would be in front of his own home, at his own gate set in the low boxwood hedge. He was there! He raised his eyes to the two-story house with attics in the roof. It looked upon him, grave and still, as if it had never known him. The eight windows in front, narrow to keep the heat in the house in winter, were as they always had been. The front door was painted green now. It had been red before, so that for a few brief weeks in the year, it would match the flowering rhododendron. That bush had grown enormously, encroaching the patch of green lawn, too big for it. The birdbath in the centre that his mother loved was still there. Why had she not taken it with her?

He could see nobody about. There was no reason to knock on the door, or to go around to the back gate. But he could go toward the church, as that was not out of bounds to anybody, and in that way be able to see the apple orchard and the small tract of farmland attached.

The church was locked. What did it matter? He was not going to go inside anyway. He had no business in a church.

CHURCHYARD

As he turned from the front door, he was facing the churchyard, with its rows of neat, old gravestones and towering old yew trees. He gulped, for a fearful thought had occurred to him. All of the Ellises were buried there. All the churchmen and their sons and wives and their deceased children. Their graves were all in a row by the gable end of the church. Were his parents even alive? With footsteps dragging, he went there, although knowing that if they had been driven out of Middledene, they might not return to be buried there.

More memories came. Happier, funny times. When he was a child he had often played in the churchyard. It had been a great place for Hide and Seek, and he smiled at the memory of ducking behind the tombs and the tall headstones, crouching low to avoid being seen by his sisters and the Harries. He had once seen a skull! The lid of a tomb had somehow lifted a little, and the wood of the coffin had rotted, revealing a whitened skull. The sight had horrified and thrilled him as if it were some forbidden sight, a glimpse into a secret world. He ran to tell his father, who had subsequently arranged for the unfortunate skeleton to be properly secured, but not until every child and probably many adults in the village had come in procession to inspect it. He had been quite famous for a while, and he had basked in it.

A woman was coming along a path. She held a simple bouquet of meadow flowers. He recognised her as Mrs. Little, Lucy's mother. She went to a grave, knelt, and laid the flowers down. Curious, Arthur took the same path and paused at the grave.

He was dismayed at the name there. Though Lucy had been an accomplice in the crime against Mr. Leamy and lied at his trial, he had, over the years, come to the conclusion that she had been the least guilty of his enemies.

LUCY ANNE LITTLE
1830-1847

Lucy! Dead at seventeen years old, dead the year after all that had happened!

He had once thought himself in love with her, but had never pursued her. It would have been unfair to have flirted with her and perhaps given her expectations, because he knew that they would not, could not marry. But Gregory Harries had no such scruples. About three weeks after Gregory had paid the visit to the Parsonage, he had seen them walking together along a woodland path, he with his arm around her. It revolted him, because Gregory would never, ever marry her. He would take what he wanted though, he was sure of that.

He decided to speak. He gave a gentle cough, and the woman turned her head toward him.

"Mrs. Little," he began, "I apologise for interrupting you."

"How do you know me?" she asked, astonished.

"I'm Arthur Ellis," he said, desperately hoping that the information would not frighten her away.

But it did not. She got to her feet, dusting her skirts down with her hand.

"Master Arthur," she said. "You have come home." There did not seem to be any animosity, or ill-will, toward the man who had been convicted of robbery and assault.

He nodded toward the inscription.

"What happened to Lucy?"

Mrs. Little looked away, as if she wished the question had not been asked.

"I'm sorry," he said.

"I will tell you, because it involves you," Mrs. Little said at last.

"Me?"

"I don't want to besmirch her memory, Mr. Ellis. Lucy was a good girl, but her head was turned by someone who ought to have known better. She fell in love with him. You know of whom I speak?"

Arthur nodded.

"You were innocent, weren't you, Mr. Ellis? You never robbed Old Man Leamy and injured him."

It felt good to have somebody know that truth. Even if it was someone who had no influence, none whatsoever, in the village and surrounding towns, and not likely to obtain him a pardon from the Queen.

"I'm going to tell you. Please don't think too badly of Lucy, as she didn't know, not at first. She thought it was a lark, a prank."

"She it was who placed my cap in Mr. Leamy's?"

"Oh no, she didn't do that. But she did take your cap, and give it to Gregory Harries, who had asked her for it, *to play a little joke on you*, he said."

There was silence.

"He, of course, promised marriage and all. Poor foolish girl! Her grandmother used to egg her on with this, telling her that her face was her fortune an' all that, but she could not turn him in. Who would listen to a serving girl anyhow, when the Harries were telling a different story?"

"What about Mr. Leamy's tin money box?" asked Arthur.

Mrs. Leamy hung her head.

"She did that, she did. Mr. Gregory came to the kitchen door and had it under his jacket. He asked her for a very big favour, and in the sweetest words and compliments, asked her to put it under your bed. She did not want to do it, but he said that it would prove her love for him, and so she did."

He considered that. It had been as he had thought, then.

"Your mother dismissed her though, for she felt she had something to do with it. She never worked another day at the Parsonage after you'd been arrested."

"How did Lucy die?" he asked, gently.

"Consumption. After Mr. Gregory suddenly upped and married, she stayed out in all weathers, not caring if she lived or died, I think."

"He married, did he? Who was the unfortunate woman who married him?"

"Oh, you know nothing, do you, Mr. Ellis? Not even about your own folks? He married your sister. They eloped."

Poor stupid Eleanor, was the thought that sprung to him.

"Do you know where the rest of my family are?"

"Not rightly, though I did hear that your father got a living in Ireland in the wildest place that was ever known, so they said."

Ireland. They were lost to him then. A journey to Ireland was beyond his means.

"Miss Susanna, she went too." Mrs. Little added, meaningfully.

He supposed that when her Captain heard of the scandal, he had ended the engagement. An army officer with any hope of promotion would not want a convict for a brother-in-law.

"Where is Mrs. Quinn?" he asked.

"She's still here, living with her sister in her cottage along the road to Streamfield. Do call on her. She was very cut up when your family left, but felt too old to go with them."

He sympathised again with Mrs. Little, and set off again through the graves toward the church, this time taking the convenient path that led from there to the Harries mansion, for use of the family and servants going to and coming from there on Sundays.

Middledene House looked exactly the same as it had before, large and imposing, as befitted the residence of the most powerful family for miles around. He looked upon it with great bitterness. Why had they destroyed him?

44

WHAT HAPPENED THAT JULY

The month had been July, a dry warm July, and it seemed to Arthur that the summer would go too fast and that he would soon have to return to school. He was enjoying his days.

After he had seen Lucy with Mr. Gregory, he had tried to put both of them out of his head. It occurred to him to tell his mother, but she would dismiss the girl. Besides, Lucy had a mother and a grandmother to guide her. She was a sweet, biddable girl. He felt some responsibility to her, he and liked her too much to see her ruined by an unscrupulous man.

One day he was going out when he came upon Gregory walking his horse past the parsonage. He fell into pace beside him.

"Gregory," he said awkwardly, for they had been on first name terms since childhood. "I wish to discuss something with you, if you will hear me."

Gregory raised his eyes upward.

"What is it?" he asked rather mockingly.

"I saw you with our serving girl," Arthur began.

"Oh, you mean Lucy, do you?"

"Yes, Lucy. I don't wish to approach her, it's not my place, and I don't want to tell my mother, in case she is dismissed, and not my sisters, so I must approach you."

"Well, what? Do you think there's something nefarious afoot?"

"She's a servant in our house, and you shouldn't be walking out with her, because you'll never marry her."

"Oh, I see." His tone was mocking. "You think I will rob her of her virtue, do you? And I wager you do not even know what that means. You're just a boy, Ellis. An awfully serious boy, too. Nobody likes serious young people. You sound like an old schoolmaster."

He allowed the insult to pass. He did not know what to say next.

"I've just had a frightful idea," said Gregory Harries. "Do you know what it is? One day I shall take my father's place, and you are expected to succeed *your* father. That thought gives me no joy at all. Of course, the living will be in my gift. I may choose whoever I wish, and if I choose you, it might be just for a year at a time perhaps."

Arthur was dumbfounded. The parish was usually bestowed for life. To keep a rector on a string from year to year was an abuse. The clergyman would probably look for a more secure tenure.

"If you don't trust my character, you won't have the living," Gregory went on. "The person whose living it is should be able to be friends with the rector. I cannot see it, Arthur. You're too serious, no fun at all. To have to invite you and your wife, whoever the dreary woman will be, regularly to the manse will be penitential. And to have to return the visit equally so."

Arthur was angry and wanted to tell him that he knew he was a thief and that he had stolen from his own mother, but he could not. He had promised Matthew.

"I'm in a hurry," Harries said then, quickly mounting his horse. "I should have been in Hempley an hour ago."

He whipped his horse and cantered away.

He had done all he could. He decided to forget about it and hope somehow that Gregory would not harm Lucy in any way.

The insults stung.

The women were inside, sewing and mending. They were talking of Susanna's wedding clothes. That was all women's business, and Arthur had no interest in it, so as the women chattered on, he did not hear a word. He put Gregory out of his mind, and tried to do the same with Lucy, though her continued presence in the parsonage added a sweetness to his life. He looked forward to seeing her every day, but he made no attempt to approach her or to allow her to know how he felt. He would miss her when he returned to school.

Then the world changed.

45
MATTHEW TROUBLED

I t was a Wednesday morning in mid-July when the quiet village stirred with rather unusual and alarming news. During the night, Mr. Leamy had been assaulted and robbed of his life savings, which he said was thirty-two pounds in gold coins, and seventy-five shillings in silver. The amount of it stunned everybody as much as the news of his assault. Everybody knew he had money, but nobody knew he was so wealthy.

"We shall visit him, Arthur," said his father.

On his way out Arthur reached his hand to the hallstand for his cap, but it was not there. He did not have time to look for it, so he went bareheaded.

The doctor was at Mr. Leamy's, bathing a wound on the back of his head.

"What happened?" asked Mr. Ellis.

"I woke very early this morning, just afore dawn. There was someone 'ere, I dint see him but I know there was someone 'ere, prying up the floorboards, he was. I got out of bed and I turned to get the poker, and then I felt a blow to my 'ead. When I awoke, the place was a shambles and my money was gone!"

Neither Arthur nor his father had noted that the house was any more of a shambles than usual, but that was irrelevant.

"You'd best move across to the inn, Mr. Leamy. You can be cared for there," said Dr. Lawson.

"Do not worry about the cost, sir. We'll have a whip-around at church next Sunday," added Mr. Ellis soothingly.

"I'm much obliged to you, Mr. Ellis. And to you, lad." Mr. Leamy nodded in Arthur's direction.

"Have you any idea who it was attacked you?" asked Dr. Lawson.

"None at all. But 'e left 'is cap after 'im. I put it away carefully to give police when they arrive. It's under my pillow."

"Best not touch the evidence any further," said Dr. Lawson. "They don't like you to touch evidence."

After he had done some rounds with his father, Arthur was free for the day. He went to the mansion where he had arranged to meet Matthew. He and all his family had been frequent callers there since childhood They knew the reception rooms, the library, and the expansive grounds almost as well as they knew their own home. Mrs. Harries and Mrs. Ellis were friends. They exchanged recipes and they discussed servants, growing herbs, and making gowns. Mr. Harries and Mr. Ellis discussed politics, farming, and speculated about the source of the Nile. Eleanor had adored Gregory all her life. Susanna was only slightly older than Matthew and Arthur, and when she was a little girl, she had often joined in their games.

There was a fine carriage outside the mansion, with a team of four excellent horses. He stopped to admire them before he mounted the steps to ring the front doorbell. Lapp, the butler, let him in. He was an old man.

"Who owns the carriage?" asked Arthur.

"That's Lord Huckle's equipage," answered Lapp. "If you wait here, Master Arthur, I will send Master Matthew to you."

Arthur stood in the front hall. It was large with old-fashioned black and white floor tiles and a sweeping staircase. The second floor had balconies that overlooked it.

"I can't come out," Matthew said abruptly when he came downstairs. He looked unhappy, a little distracted.

"I thought we were going fishing," said Arthur.

"Can't. The magistrate is here. In any case, my brother wants to borrow my tackle, because he's going to Skegness with his friends."

"So, he got the money then," Arthur said in a conspiratorial whisper.

Silence fell and Arthur knew that the subject of Gregory's finances was a sticky one, so he said no more.

Mrs. Harries appeared at one of the railings upstairs.

"Matthew?" she called, in a strange, tense tone that Arthur had never heard her use before.

"I must go," said Matthew quickly.

Arthur left, hands in his pockets, puzzled.

He decided to go to the mill, where he liked to watch the wheels turning and the water flowing underneath.

46
LORD HUCKLE

He had just reached the millstream when he heard his name called. He turned around to see Susanna catching up with him at a run. She was in bad humour.

"I've been looking for you everywhere," she scolded Arthur. "You're to come back to the house directly. Papa wants you."

"What's the matter?" asked Arthur.

"I don't know," was Susanna's cross answer. "It's *hot* and I had to *run*. Lord Huckle called upon Papa, and he sent me to fetch you. Mrs. Greene saw you going in this direction, so I guessed you were coming here. Where's Matthew?" she asked, in a calmer tone, falling into pace beside him as they turned for the village.

"He wouldn't come out. Lord Huckle was there when I called, and Mrs. Harries acted strange, calling Matthew away while he was speaking to me. I don't know what it is."

"Gregory must be in trouble again," said Susanna with contempt. "I wish I could get Eleanor to stop thinking about him. She's making a fool of herself."

Lord Huckle's carriage and team looked very grand outside the parsonage gate. Many visitors of note who called to the Mansion also called upon his father. Perhaps his father wished him to become acquainted with these kinds of people, since he was to succeed him. He knew he would be expected to be attired appropriately, so after letting himself in, he ran upstairs to change from his rough play costume into his good trousers and shirt. However, his father came out of the front parlour and called him to come down directly, as he was. He looked agitated, and Arthur looked at him with surprise.

"Here he is," his father said, laying a hand on his shoulder as they entered the parlour. "Lord Huckle, may I present my son, Arthur Ellis. I'm sure there is an innocent explanation for all this, my Lord."

Mrs. Ellis was in the parlour also. She got up from her chair and stood by her son's side. His sisters were not present. Arthur looked from one parent to another, bewildered.

"Just a few questions for you, my boy," said Lord Huckle, who was seated in the best chair, though it was too small for his ample corporation. "Where were you last night?"

"I was at home last night," Arthur answered, puzzled.

"All night, lad?"

"Yes, all night."

"You did not go out at all?"

"No, not at all, sir."

There was silence.

"You see, lad, if you did go out after dark last night, when your parents thought you to be abed and asleep, it would be better for you to say so now." Lord Huckle scratched his ear.

"But I was not out, sir."

"No, he was not out!" said his mother.

"Madam, if you would kindly leave this to me," said Lord Huckle. "Master Arthur, a very serious thing happened in the village last night. Do you know what it was?"

Arthur remembered then that Lord Huckle was the magistrate for the district.

"Yes, I do. Mr. Leamy was robbed, and hit over the head with something."

"How do you know he was hit over the head, in particular?"

"With respect, Lord Huckle, we have been to see him," his father put in. "Besides, the entire village knows that Mr. Leamy was hit over the head."

"Do they? A small village, I suppose, has nothing to do but gossip. I should have thought the clergy were above that. Well, Arthur, do you know anything more about Mr. Leamy?"

"About what happened to him? No, sir."

"Did you know he had money, Arthur?"

"Yes, sir. Everybody knew that, too."

Lord Huckle shoved a plump hand into his pocket and drew out a crumpled piece of grubby, navy worsted which he shook out.

"That's my cap!" exclaimed Arthur.

"Are you sure this is your cap, Master Arthur?"

"Yes, sir. It is mine, I looked for it this morning and it was gone."

"Where did you lose it, Arthur?"

"I don't know, sir. I hung it up on the hallstand last night and it wasn't there this morning."

"Mr. Ellis, I do not like to put this question to you, but does your boy tell lies?"

"He does not, my Lord. Arthur does not lie." Mr. Ellis looked aggravated.

"This cap was found in Mr. Leamy's cabin, my boy, and has already been identified as yours. You were also seen leaving the cabin just before dawn this morning."

"No, that's not true. I don't know how it got there," Arthur said, frowning. "Honestly, Mama and Papa, I haven't been in his house for days now, until this morning when Papa and I went there."

"Might I ask who claims to have seen my son, and who identified the cap as his?" asked Mr. Ellis.

"That is *sub judice*," said Lord Huckle. "I may not divulge it. I will need to search the house, Mr. Ellis."

"If you must, I have no objection to it," Mr. Ellis said testily. Mrs. Ellis was flushing with indignation. She sat down rather weakly in the nearest chair.

The footman was summoned, and he went to call the constables, who were refreshing themselves at the inn. The family was ordered to keep to the parlour, and from there they could hear footsteps and scrapes and thuds. Lord Huckle sat with them.

"I had nothing to do with Mr. Leamy's robbery, Father," said Arthur, who was beginning to fit everything together in his head.

"We know you hadn't, son."

It suddenly ran into Arthur's mind, like a flash of lightening, who could have done this. But it was a preposterous thought! Should he tell his mother and father that Master Gregory was a thief? And that he had money today that he did not have before? He could not. He had promised Matthew.

He could not. He had promised Matthew.

The constables came downstairs. One carried a small tin box.

"This, sir, is what we found in Master Ellis' room. I think you should see the contents." The constable opened it.

"Five silver coins. Where's the rest of it, boy?" spluttered the Lord, as Mrs. Ellis began to weep. "Where have you hidden the gold and the rest of the silver? Own up, and we may be merciful!"

"I never saw that before in my life," cried Arthur.

"Arrest him," Lord Huckle said, heaving his bulk out of the chair.

"My Lord, I beg you!" shouted his father.

"If you will pardon the expression, Reverend, he is guilty as sin," said the magistrate. "The evidence is overwhelming, and there is more that I have not produced yet. He will be tried at the Michaelmas Assizes in Hempley. Take him out, lads. Tomorrow I will send a team to search the outbuildings, for he has hidden that fortune somewhere."

"No, no! Please, sir, no! I did not rob Mr. Leamy!"

His shouts were in vain.

His mother was screaming, his father was shouting, his sisters came running, shrieking. Arthur found his hands tied behind his back, and he was marched out between two constables towards the gate.

They pushed him onto a cart hired from a villager. He twisted himself around to see his mother and father and sisters running after him, crying and shouting. Some of the neighbours had come from their houses and were rooted to the ground, staring at the scene.

Lucy was at the front door of his home, her face frozen with horror.

The cart rounded a bend and he had never beheld his home from that day until this.

47

WHERE EVIL LURKS

The cell he was held in was like a coal hole with a slab for a bed. In spite of the warm weather outside, it was chilly and damp. He was given mouldy bread and a mug of water.

"This is a big mistake," he told himself as he tried to sleep. *"I will be out tomorrow. Everybody in the village knows I'm not the culprit. They must know. Mr. Harries will speak for me. He will tell the magistrate that he's known me all my life and that I'm innocent."*

His heart rose in the morning when the cell door was unlocked and he was told to follow the guard. Was his father here to take him home? To his dismay, he was pushed into a van and taken away from the police station, along with a few other prisoners.

He was transferred to another prison on Bank Street. He had heard of this place. It was a medieval building that had been built over a river, in such a way that the water-closets in the cells could be emptied straight into it. There was a dreadful smell, and there were rats running everywhere.

There seemed to be some sort of argument between the wardens as he was marched down a hallway.

"You can't put this young fellow in with the Brute. Chesser was supposed to go in with 'im. He's a boxer, is Chesser."

"I 'ave orders, don't I?"

"If you 'ave orders, we know why. Money changed 'ands. But it isn't right, it isn't right."

He was shoved into a cell with a large tough man, the said Brute. He was afraid to sleep, but exhaustion overcame him. He awoke in total darkness to someone dragging him from his pallet. He was thrown about the cell. He tried to defend himself, but was no match for the Brute. Other prisoners joined their shouts to his. Every possible violence was done to him before the wardens unlocked the cell door.

He was carried away on a stretcher, and seen by a surgeon. Three broken bones were set, and wounds that had been inflicted by a sharp piece of something. stone perhaps, were stitched. He felt that he had been in Hell and had met Satan. He spent a week in the hospital and then was taken to a cell of his own.

Thoughts circled endlessly in his mind like vultures over a dying animal. Where was God? He felt abandoned by God. He had done nothing to deserve this! He could never go back to being the carefree lad he was before. Even if he were set free this minute, he was a different person, broken and angry. He could never be the same.

His bones healed, and his mother and father were allowed to visit. He still had bruises aplenty, so he told them he fell. Their hearts were already broken, and he could not burden them with the news that he had been grievously assaulted.

Summer faded into autumn. His father had engaged counsel for him, and Arthur, broken in spirit and knowing that the allegation against him was very serious, had reluctantly decided to break his promise to Matthew and had told Mr. Savidge all.

His trial came at last, held in the large courtyard of the Mallard Arms. The judge was a wigged and somber-looking chap named Portering. The courtyard was jammed. Lesser cases were heard first and disposed of, and then it was Arthur's turn.

His father and mother attended. They looked thin and pale. Both held small Bibles in their hands. How could they still believe in all that? Arthur thought, not in anger, but rather pitying them.

"Where is the victim?" asked Judge Portering.

The Prosecutor, a man named Mr. Farley, stood. "He is unwell and unable to give evidence, my Lord. But we do not need him to be present. I have his testimony."

"Let us hear it," said the judge. "Jury, pay attention."

The Prosecutor narrated the crime and the statement taken from Mr. Leamy, and the evidence that had led to Arthur Ellis' arrest.

"A clergyman's son? We shall see about that," said the Judge. He looked rather doubtful and Arthur's heart lifted for a while.

The witnesses were called, as well asthe constables upon the scene, and Arthur listened to every word. It was simply a rehash of the testimony.

"Any more?" asked the judge, crossly. It was nearly time for luncheon and he could smell roast beef.

"Yes, my Lord. I will call Master Matthew Harries to the witness stand."

Matthew! Matthew was going to testify! Surely not against him? Matthew had been his friend all of his life.

Then he saw Matthew walking in. He looked straight ahead of him, and did not look at him at all, while he took the witness stand.

"Can you tell us, Master Harries, if you know Master Ellis?"

"Yes, sir."

"In what way, Master Harries?"

"We were friends, sir."

"Good friends?"

"Yes, sir."

"What did you do together?"

"We went about the woods and fields, and went fishing. And we played games, sir."

"Do you see Master Arthur Ellis in this court, Master Harries?"

Matthew looked in his direction. Their eyes met for a split second only before Matthew withdrew his.

"Yes, sir. He is the prisoner in the dock, sir."

"Very well. Now would you like to tell us what happened in the days preceding the robbery at the blacksmith's house?"

"We went fishing one day, sir, and caught a trout. On the way home, Arthur, Master Ellis, said he was going to give it to Mr. Leamy."

"And?"

"And he added that Mr. Leamy had pots of money hidden away."

Arthur gripped the railing in front of him.

"No," he said, though his Counsel had told him strongly not to say anything.

"The prisoner will be silent," said Judge Portering, glaring at him.

"He said that he knew where it was hidden."

Arthur shook his head in despair. He bit back tears. He looked imploringly at his parents. They did not believe any of this, did they?

"Was anybody else witness to this conversation, Master Harries?"

"Yes, sir." Matthew seemed to hesitate. "My older brother, sir. He caught up with us and dismounted his horse and walked with us."

"And the prisoner said all this in your and in your brother's presence?"

"Yes, he did, sir."

"Anything else, Master Harries?"

"A few days later, he asked me to help him to steal it. I said no. I didn't think he was really going to do it, sir; I thought it was all talk. I'm sorry now that I didn't tell my father."

Arthur was horrified by now. This betrayal was worse than anything he had experienced, even in the prison cell where he had been a punchbag for the Brute. It tore his soul.

The cross-examination was tough, but nothing would budge Matthew from his story.

"I have no more questions," said Mr. Savidge.

"You may stand down," said the Judge to Matthew.

The aroma of roast beef could no longer be ignored. The judge hammered his gavel.

"The court will recess. We will resume at two o'clock," he rapped.

48

SENTENCING

There was no roast beef for Arthur. He gulped a watery soup and bread in the holding cell at the police station while he tried to make sense of Matthew's testimony. The Brute was in the same cell and grinned at him with several teeth missing. Thankfully there was a guard in attendance all the time, and other prisoners there also. All the same, Matthew had to force himself to finish the soup and bread.

He remembered how odd Matthew had acted when he had called for him that day, how he had fidgeted and seemed out of sorts. And his mother at the upstairs railings sternly calling him away.

They knew Gregory had committed the crime. And they all banded together to protect him.

The magistrate had visited the Harries house before coming to arrest him, and the family must have found out by then that it had been Gregory who had robbed Mr. Leamy. Gregory would have told them not to worry, that he had planted Arthur Ellis' cap there. What evil! Why had they not told the magistrate the truth? Why did they go along with him, and not only that, to make it even worse, concocted lies to nail it on an innocent person? The wickedness was beyond his understanding. In the afternoon, when it was his turn to give a defense, he would tell them all! The jury would believe him, they would. He was a clergyman's son and had never stolen anything in his life.

The wickedness was beyond his understanding. In the afternoon, when it was his turn to give a defense, he would tell them all! The jury would believe him, they would. He was a clergyman's son and had never stolen anything in his life.

Court resumed. But the Court had two more witness to call. Eben Stack was a simple shepherd. He took the stand trembling, and said that he saw a young man leaving the blacksmith's house around five o'clock in the morning. He was tall. He was carrying something.

Arthur's heart lightened. He was not tall! However, when the Prosecutor pressed Eben on this, he grew confused and said he might have been wrong about the height. It might have been a smaller man than what he had thought at first. He could not remember anything about the height, in truth, and he agreed that it was only half-light. He rushed from the stand when dismissed, as if he had been made to stand on flaming embers.

Court resumed. But the prosecution had one more witness to call, Mr. Gregory Harries.

Impeccably dressed in a black jacket, black bowtie, and top hat, he carried a gold-tipped cane and cut quite a dashing figure as he mounted the stand. He pulled off his white gloves. His expression was serious and somber, and he looked with indulgence and kindness toward the Jury.

In his answers, in which he supported all his young brother said, he conveyed an air of deep sorrow and regret at having to agree. Yes, that was said. He had been surprised to hear a clergyman's son, of all people, talk so blandly of the poor smithy, but he regretted to say that it was so. The cross-examination was very respectful, and Arthur felt that Mr. Savidge was intimidated by Gregory's rank and his appearance.

With two persons of rank giving evidence against him, what chance did he have?

It was Arthur's turn to give evidence. He was angry now, deeply resentful and angry. He refuted what the two brothers had said.

"It was Mr. Gregory, not me, who said all that about the smithy. He was short of money. Matthew told me he was in debt and that he and his father had endless rows about it. He wanted to go away with his friends, he wanted to buy a carriage and a team, he wanted everything his friends had. He planted my cap, I bet he asked our maid, Lucy, because they were sweethearts."

The Prosecutor sprang to his feet.

"Objection! My Lord, Mr. Harries is not the person on trial here."

"Indeed he is not," said Judge Portering. "There will be no more evidence along that line, Mr. Ellis. But perhaps we need to hear from this maidservant, Lucy."

And so the trial went on for the following day. A trembling Lucy took the stand. She looked terrified and refused to raise her head.

No, she knew nothing about the cap, never even noticed whether it was there on the peg. No, she never saw that tin box before. No, she did not know Mr. Gregory Harries. She had never spoken to him except to serve him tea once in the parsonage and ask him how much sugar.

Arthur felt as if he had entered a world that was unreal, a world that made no sense.

The judge seemed very sympathetic to the pretty little maid, and when Mr. Savidge began to cross-examine her, reducing her to tears, Mr. Farley made so many objections, he acceded to every one. The jury huddled in a corner, and twenty minutes later were ready to give their verdict. Arthur watched them carefully. What were their faces saying, with their eyes cast down? Who had they believed? Him, or the witnesses arrayed against him?

Arthur Ellis was guilty. The news numbed him.

The judge pronounced sentence. He was to be transported for seven years to Van Diemen's Land. The judge had a great deal more to say, and it stung. A clergyman's only son, a disgrace to his good parents, a disgrace to the Church of England. It was a bad, bad case, and if the victim had died, he would have had no option but to hang him. He could sentence him to penal servitude for life, but would not, on account of his afflicted parents, good people surely, who had had the misfortune of producing a bad seed, who would bear this disgrace for the rest of their lives. It was on their account that he was being lenient, for he could haveimprisoned him for life.

Arthur was taken away, loudly protesting his innocence, until he was thrown into the cell. He lay there in the darkness, sprawled, and pounded his fists on the hard concrete for a long, long time.

His life was over. He was sixteen years old and was ruined, he might as well have been hanged. His parents and sisters were allowed to see him before he was taken to the convict ship, and they said little, but wept.

After his conversation with Mrs. Little, Arthur left the churchyard and turned his steps towards a small side-road up a hill and came to a row of small cottages. If his memory was correct, Mrs. Quinn's sister lived in the second one, so he unlatched the gate and went to the door.

It opened before he had time to knock. A familiar, beloved old face peered out.

"It is you! Oh, thank God you are safely returned!" Mrs. Quinn enjoined, pulling him in toward her for an embrace. "Mrs. Little just told me you were here! You have no place to stay, I'm sure, and by the looks of you, you could do with a bite to eat. Do you remember my sister, Babs, Miss Miller?"

An older woman arose from her seat by the fire.

He was ushered to a chair by the table and sat down. Soon, there was a pot of tea brewing and a plate of bread and jam set before him.

"It's not much, Master Arthur. But you shall have a good breakfast tomorrow morning."

"Are you sure you have room for me overnight?"

"Of course we have room for you, Master Arthur. After all your family meant to me, how could you ask me that?"

"Have you ever heard from them, Mrs. Quinn?"

In answer, she rose and went to the dresser, where she opened a drawer and took out a large packet.

"These are all letters for you," she said. "They sent them 'ere when they realised you mustn't have been getting theirs. They thought you'd come back to England."

He took the precious packet and opened it, there fell out several letters, some with his father's handwriting, others with his mother's.

"Thank you," was all he could manage to say, with a voice choking with emotion.

"We go early to bed, so you can stay up and read them. You don't mind sleeping in the settle bed here in the kitchen?"

"If you knew the kinds of beds I've had in the last seven years, you'd know that to me, a settle bed is the last word in luxury," he said.

As he drank his hot tea, his precious packet of letters by his side, he asked if they could tell them anything about Mr. Leamy.

"I was always wondering if he thought I did it," he said. "It troubled me. He liked me, and he did not like many people."

Mrs. Quinn poured him more tea and spooned sugar into it.

"He knew who did it," she said. "After he had recovered from the blow, he remembered more about the night that he was robbed."

"What did he remember?" Arthur exclaimed.

"As soon as he heard that you had been arrested, he began to say that it was not you. He was certain of it."

"And what happened then?"

"Certain people were afraid that the next thing he would say was that he knew who did it, so they took pains to hush him up, they did! I'll tell you summat else, Master Arthur. He's not mad. They had him declared mad though, and sent to the asylum."

Arthur made no reaction.

"What, you don't seem surprised, Master Arthur."

"Nothing surprises me, I'm afraid. I've seen so much evil now, here in England, and in that place where I had to spend seven years. Who declared him insane? How did they do it?"

"As soon as he began to say it wan't you, the Harries took charge of 'im. They took him out of the inn, where he was getting the best of care, and up to the Manse he was carried, supposedly to give him the best money could offer, and there, they began to report that 'e was doing all sorts of odd things, and so Dr. Lawson certified him and off he went to the Asylum in Hempley, and that was ever afore your trial."

"They took care of everything," he said bitterly. "Does anybody know where Matthew is?"

"No, but they say he took your sentencing very hard. You are not out for revenge or anything, are you, Master Arthur?"

"All I want is to clear my name," was his reply, not really knowing if that was the truth, and soon the women made their way to bed, leaving him with the good candle.

50

LETTERS

Arthur arranged the letters on the table and read them from the beginning. It had been eighteen months before the family had realised that he might not be receiving any letters from them, so the first one was a brief summary of what had happened after he had parted from them.

'We returned home the night you were sentenced, to find a mob outside our door. They jeered at us. People we had known, served, and loved for years, turned completely against us. Mrs. Quinn was in the doorway, a rolling pin in her hand, determined to defend us. Mr. Harries sent a note to say that my services were no longer required, we were to be gone within a week. Thankfully, a friend with whom I had studied knew of a living nobody else in the British Isles wanted, in County Kerry on the edge of the

Atlantic Ocean. We had a very bad journey from the seaport, rocky ground, wheels sticking in mud, gales, hungry people everywhere begging for crusts. You must have heard of the famine. Upon arrival not even a fire had been lit to welcome us, for nobody knew when we were to arrive. The population of Dunquale had been deeply affected by the potato blight. The suffering was unimaginable, and we buried our own sorrows to help the afflicted Irish, working in soup kitchens...' So the first years of their sojourn in Ireland was sketched for him.

But what of Eleanor? He wondered. Ah, there. His father had kept the sad news until the very last. *'The morning before we left the parsonage, she was gone, and a note left to say that she had eloped with Mr. Harries. I went up to the Mansion and was not received. There was no opportunity for pursuit. We have not heard of them since and have no idea if the marriage took place or not. We hope so. And then there is poor Susanna. When she wrote to Captain Wright from Ireland, he made no reply. Another letter went sailing off, again with no reply. She concluded that she was jilted, and in time, he wrote a stiff note stating that he did not know when he would be in a position to marry, etc., etc., inviting her to break the engagement. How few friends we have when we meet misfortune. We hold steadfast to the knowledge that you are innocent and have been done a great injustice by those we regarded as our dear friends, and it offends us all the more that Eleanor went off with that villain. But gold is tested in fire. Your mother and I pray that you have remained steadfast in this time, son.'*

It was many years since he had heard that phrase. What testing! What fire! Hotter than a furnace!

The next letters were more general, but one contained the interesting news that Susanna was married to a Kerryman, a man with an estate of one hundred acres. She was Mrs. Deegan.

The other letters contained news of a fine boy grandchild, and then another. He was an uncle. No word had come from Eleanor. They all loved Ireland now. The views from their house were spectacular, the walks provided splendid vistas, and they would not wish to be anywhere else. Would he come over to live with them? Nobody here knew their particular history, except Mr. Deegan. But he was such a good, kind-hearted sort, and loved Susanna very much, it had not made a difference. The grandchildren, John and Arthur, were the joy of their lives, now.

Arthur, he smiled. He hoped that Arthur would be more fortunate in life than his uncle of the same name.

The candle was burning low as he read this, the last letter. No, he would not go to Ireland, even if he had the money. He still had to clear his name. He wished to meet the Harries. All of them. He had to get them to confess.

As he closed his eyes to sleep, the words "gold is tested in fire" seemed to whisper in his ear. It may be so, but he had failed the test. He was not gold. His father, on the other hand, was. A prayer almost sprung to his lips for the second time that day, but he turned from it.

51

MIDDLEDENE HOUSE REVISITED

rthur walked up to the front door of Middledene House and pulled the bell. He heard it resound inside, the same sound as when he had been a boy. It was answered by Lapp, who looked upon him with great annoyance and suspicion.

"Get yourself around to the back door if you have any business here." he said roughly.

"Do you not know me, Lapp?" Arthur took off his battered hat and ran his hands through his mop of thick, wheat-coloured hair.

The butler's face turned several colours, but settled on deathly white.

"Arthur Ellis! You've come back! You've come back."
He trembled as if he were perceiving a ghost. He
made as if to shut the door but Arthur was too quick
for him and burst inside, into the grand hallway with
the black and white chessboard tiles and heavy old-
fashioned furniture.

Seven years of penal servitude had stripped him of
polite society's requirement to exercise courtesy
towards one's betters.

"Mr. Harries! Where are you?" he shouted to the
galleries and rooms above. "This is Arthur Ellis, and
I demand an interview this moment! I will not leave
until I am satisfied! You may call the magistrate. You
may call out the army if you choose! But I will
speak!"

He heard a door squeak open upstairs, and an old
man shuffled out of the room he remembered to be
the library. He planted his two hands on the railing
overlooking the massive hall, and stared at him in
astonishment. From another part of the gallery, an
older woman emerged, her face pale with fright. It
was Mrs. Harries.

Arthur calmed as the old couple descended the
stairs. He realised he would get no good from them
if he was belligerent.

"I'm entitled to know what happened," he said. "May we speak in private?"

They led the way to the drawing room. He looked about him before sitting down. It looked exactly the same as he remembered, except that the furnishings had gotten old and shabby.

"Brandy?" offered Mr. Harries rather timidly.

"No, thank you." Arthur did not trust himself to act with reason and calm if he drank.

The old man helped himself to a brandy, his hands shaking.

Mrs. Harries was looking at her feet. Her hands were tightly clasped in her lap. Her shoulders shook a little. Was she crying?

Mr. Harries seated himself in his chair and gulped the brandy.

"What brings you here?" he asked abruptly.

"I'm going to clear my name," said Arthur slowly and evenly. This was met with silence.

"You all lied, didn't you? Every one of you? Even before my arrest, you knew who had taken Mr. Leamy's money, and you were determined that your son and heir would not suffer for it, as he deserved.

But I believe you are related to me now, much as I dislike the connection."

The couple looked at one another. Was it possible they did not know? They surely must.

"Gregory and my sister Eleanor," said Arthur testily.

Mr. Harries cleared his throat. "It did not happen," he said. "They eloped, but the marriage did not occur."

"So my sister, along with me, has been violated by this family! Her reputation is in ruins. Where is she?"

"If you please, Arthur. My wife is very upset. We have suffered too, you know."

"Not as much as we have. Where is my sister Eleanor?"

"We do not know," sobbed Mrs. Harries. "Will you please leave this house? What is there to be gained by speaking of all this? I wish we had left Gregory to his fate, for we have nobody now."

"At least tell me, where is Matthew?"

"That we do not know either, but the last we heard, he was in Nottingham. He sent us a note to tell us that he was alive and well, and that we were not to try to find him."

There was silence following this for a few moments.

"We would like to offer you some restitution for the wrong we have done you," Mr. Harries said stiffly, getting up from his chair.

"No, I don't want money. All I want is my good name. I want you to go to the magistrate and make a statement that you lied, and your family lied, to protect Gregory."

"That we will never do," said Mr. Harries quietly. He pulled the bell.

En route to Nottingham, he went through Hempley, where he went to visit Mr. Leamy. The asylum ward of the workhouse was a sad place. Some patients were tied to chairs, others roamed around aimlessly, and one man was singing *"D'ye ken John Peel, with his coat so gray, d'ye ken John Peel at the break of the day'* over and over, but Mr. Leamy seemed composed and in his right mind. He was sitting in a chair by the window. He remembered him well and shook his hand.

"Young Mr. Harries took my life savings, you know." He said loud and clear, unafraid of being heard by anybody. "I can say anything I like in here," he added somewhat gleefully. "I can say it ten times a day if I like. Mr. Ellis, will you help me to get it back from young Mr. Harries? I will gladly give you half. The remainder I will use for a comfortable home for myself, with a servant to look after me."

"I will try, Mr. Leamy. But I fear the prospect is poor. He may have spent it all, you know. But if I find him, I will do my best."

He continued north, and he reached Nottingham near dark two days later. It was dominated by a castle, and its large market square had evidence of a busy day with vendors taking down stalls. He watched his step to avoid the rotten fruit on the ground, though he spied a good apple and pocketed it after wiping it with his cuff. He had very little money.

He toured the public houses in search of Matthew. Nobody knew of him, but a man thought he remembered a young man *"named Harris"* who spoke posh, got drunk frequently, and said that he could never go home again, but wouldn't say why. He then met with some kind of accident. He'd gone to the hospital, and from there, he went off and said he was joining a monastery or some such.

"Are there monasteries nearby?" asked Arthur.

"Not that I know of, since Henry the Eight," chuckled the informant. "The place they call the friary is not a friary now."

"There's someplace in Sherwood Forest," put in the barman. "A group of foreigners went out there some years ago to pray. They sometimes come into town to beg, and most of what they get, they give to the poor."

"You mean the Sherwood Forest of Robin Hood?" asked Arthur.

"What other Sherwood Forest is there?" said the barman.

53

SHERWOOD

He had no other ideas, so he decided to go to the monks of Sherwood Forest. A few inquiries in villages along the way were fruitful. The monks were called Brothers of St. Francis, and they lived in a few buildings on the northern edge of the forest, away from the world, there to pray, grow vegetables and provide hospitality to strangers.

He had been advised to go around by road to reach his destination, but the appeal of Sherwood Forest was strong, so he went through it, with the express purpose of viewing the Major Oak. It did not disappoint. It was magnificent with a high and spreading canopy. Its majesty took his breath away. Looking at this tree, he felt small and humble. He wanted to thank Whoever had put it there, but since he was not speaking to God, there was nobody to thank.

As darkness fell, it became very cold. He sat down on a dry patch of brush and pulled a piece of bread from his pocket, another apple, and a flask of water given him by the barman, who had been a good sort. He burrowed under a pile of leaves, where he did not sleep well because of the cold, but awoke to birdsong in the morning. He'd slept in the outdoors many times and had often been colder than this, but he had never awakened in one of Nature's Cathedrals. He again marveled, and this time, he found himself saying, quite deliberately, *"Thank you, God. Thank you. It's marvelous, and You must be marvelous also."*

A spirit rushed over him, so strong and insistent, a certainty that he was loved, and had always been, even in his worst, bitterest moments, even when he had suffered horribly at the hands of the Brute and later at the overseers' cruelty in Van Diemens Land. Loved! It was so strong it almost overwhelmed him, so that he fell on his knees and wept.

God had been waiting for him to turn to Him. It was true then, that if you take one step toward God, He will take ninety-nine. He felt overwhelmed for a long time, until the sun was shining weakly through the tree-tops.

He had nothing to eat, so he set off after a drink of water. All was silent, and the leaves whirled about him, and then snowflakes began to fall. He was in a blizzard now. He did not know where he was going. Was he going around in circles? The hours wore on. It had stopped snowing, but he had no idea if it was late morning or afternoon. Hungry and freezing, he at last leaned up against the trunk of a broad tree and considered that he was hopelessly lost. The conviction that he was loved was still with him. If he died here, it would be all right, he thought. It would be a good place to pass away. He'd asked God's forgiveness for his sins and experienced a loving presence all day long. He was meant to die this very day.

Gold is tested in fire. He had lost his faith, but now it was back. Perhaps now that he had proved himself Gold after all, it was time for him to die. He was content to do so. He was even longing to leave the troubles of this world behind him. He would welcome it.

. . .

He heard faraway voices chanting as he crumpled to the ground.

54

SHERWOOD ABBEY

He was in a white room now, in a simple room with curtains on the windows, and a white chair and table. A log fire blazed. It was very, very quiet. He lay there. This was Heaven, then? But a burning pain rushed through his feet. There wasn't supposed to be pain in Heaven!

"I'm still on earth," he said rather glumly.

"Is it you, Arthur? I am sure it is you." said a familiar voice. And a face he recognised looked over him, older, pale, and hollow-cheeked, but unmistakable.

"Matthew Harries!" he said.

He had not planned their meeting to be like this. He had rehearsed what he wanted to say, the words had been chosen, but now everything had changed.

"I want to say I'm sorry, Arthur." Matthew spoke in a rush. "I've wanted to say it for years and years. They made me do it, and I couldn't stand up to them. Father said it would kill Mother if Gregory was put away, and he'd hold me responsible for her death. What I did is eating me alive."

Arthur struggled to sit up.

"You were so calm about it on the stand," he remarked.

"They rehearsed me, over and over."

"It was a rough place. See this here?" he passed his hand over the scar on his cheek. "A fellow went after me with a knife. I have a collection of scars in fact. First ones, in prison in Hempley. The murderer they named the Brute. They put me in with him."

Matthew looked to one side, ashamed.

"Sorry, old fellow. No really, I can't tell you how sorry."

"The fishing was good out there," Arthur said after a moment. "Orange Roughy. It's a white fish, tasty. I think it's perch, here."

"So, do you forgive me?"

"Yes. But what are you doing here? You're not Roman Catholic. Or are they Anglican? My feet are killing me. What's the matter with them?"

"You were frozen when we found you. Now the circulation is coming back. Friar Pacelli put some balm on them. Friar Ivanovich is getting you some soup. Friar Marx said he doesn't want to amputate your toes because his saw is rusty. He was a surgeon at Waterloo under the Prussian fellow Blucher."

"My toes will stay attached to my foot, thank you! Are they all foreigners? Are you one of them now?"

"No. They won't take me. I do odd jobs. I do the garden and sweep the rooms and I'm learning how to cook. They don't eat meat. Only fish now and then."

The door opened and he fell silent. A monk clad in brown robes was coming in with a tray of soup and bread. Arthur found it amusing that he and Matthew gestured to each other instead of speaking. Was the monk deaf, or did he not speak English? Then he remembered his father telling him that monks often kept silent for most of the day, so that they could hear the Divine speak to them in their hearts.

The pain lasted for an hour or so, then abated. He could feel his toes again. He was not about to complain to Brother Marx when he came in to inspect them. The old fellow looked like he could hardly make out his toes, never mind see to amputate them.

The following day, he was able to sit out by the fire for a while. Matthew sat in the other chair. Arthur gave him news about the Ellises in Ireland, but the conversation was strained. Matthew was uneasy and unhappy.

"I want to clear your name," he burst out at last. "Even if they find Gregory and put him away, I want to go to the police and make a sworn statement."

"Would you? Would you, really? Do you have any idea where Gregory is?"

"No. He could be in America for all I know."

"Do you know anything about my sister Eleanor?"

Matthew bit his lip and looked away in embarrassment.

"You do. Tell me. I need to know."

"I met her a year ago, in Nottingham. She's ruined. She's a fallen woman, an unfortunate."

Arthur was stunned at this news. It hit him with great horror. *But she deserves it*, was his unbidden, angry thought, because her love for Gregory had not abated one whit by what he had done to her own family.

"I offered to marry her," Matthew said, looking up suddenly with eyes wide and sincere. "To make her respectable because my family had been responsible for her ruin. But she turned me down. She wasn't that much older than me, only four years. We could have been happy if we had put our minds to it."

"That was decent of you," Arthur said. He thought suddenly of Caroline Davey, the young, unhappy Caroline Davey.

"She said she was going to London, where she was unknown. She was afraid of being recognised in the north country."

MIDWINTER JOURNEY

rthur stayed at the monastery for two months, a great deal longer than he had anticipated. But the weather was too bad to set out on a long journey, especially when he would have to walk most of the way. After he had recovered his strength, he earned his keep by chopping wood, mending robes and furnishings, and doing other odd jobs.

"Your friend Mr. Harries," said Father Abbott one day as he was feeding the hens. "He is a troubled man. He has told me your history. You came here to ask him to clear your name, did you not?"

"Yes, but I do not know if he will do it, even though he says he is willing."

Father Abbott nodded and went upon his way, reading prayers from his book.

After Matthew's initial declaration about going to the police, he had said nothing more upon the subject. Of course, it would ruin his life and that of his parents to confess now. Arthur thought that he might put it off because the harm to himself might outweigh clearing Arthur's name. If Matthew made a legal statement saying he had committed perjury, he could suffer the same fate as he, probably not as harsh, but considering the injustice done, he could be thrown into prison for a year or two.

"I'm going to have to leave, too, in the spring." Matthew said to him dolefully the day before he was to set out. "Father Abbott says I'm hiding out here, and this isn't a refuge for people hiding from the world. I have to face the real world and do something for myself. They don't like how I am cutting my parents, and they won't let me join while I've done nothing to right the wrong I did to you."

"And are you going to do it?" Arthur asked bluntly.

Matthew looked down. "Not yet," he said.

"I see," Arthur said tersely. "You said you would. I can't get any kind of situation without this crime being scrubbed clean from my history. You know that, don't you?"

"Yes, of course, but you could go back out there and become a sheep farmer…" Matthew's voice trailed off.

Arthur walked away, angry. In Matthew's mind then, there was no necessity for him to come clean, because he, Arthur, could always emigrate and become a sheep farmer.

He left the following day, and Matthew was nowhere to be seen as he said goodbye.

Why were people so weak when it came to doing the right thing?

At least he did not have to walk all the way back to London. Father Abbott had given him the train fare.

56

A FRIEND IN MR. ELLIS

Caroline was watched whenever she went out. The bawds kept their girls in such a state of terror that none dared to escape. She longed to return to Cheapside just to see her old home. She dreamed of taking an omnibus and alighting near the church, and gazing at the parsonage from across the street, well hidden in case somebody came out. But she never did. She thought of writing, but they were not allowed to have pen and paper.

She was happy to see Mr. Ellis back again. He had a calm air, and always spoke sensibly, weighing his words before he spoke. She thought he had a high degree of understanding and was very wise. It astonished her that he was interested in her as a person and wanted to see her at liberty again. But their meetings were awkward, speaking in hushed tones in her room, and she knew he could not afford to pay to have to see her.

"You must get away before it's too late," he urged her.

"When will it be too late?"

"When you become like the others, when you are so entrenched in this life that you forget you had another, or you can have another."

"But what can I do?" she asked desperately.

"I don't know yet," he said. He had no ideas. He could not offer marriage, as he was still living hand to mouth. Besides, she was too young to make up her mind about who she wished to marry.

Perhaps he should have taken the money from Master Harries, but pride had not allowed him to.

"They'll harm my family if I escape," she said.

"It might be an empty threat," he mused, speaking after a moment. "They don't want to come to the attention of the police just for the sake of one girl escaping them. I rather think they'd do nothing at all."

"Do you really think so?"

"Yes, I do."

"Then I will leave here!" she jumped to her feet. "I will be free! But back to Cheapside, I cannot do that. I'm too ashamed. No, I shall make my own way."

"I will find out what I can," he promised, not having any idea how to go about it.

"Thank you, Mr. Ellis. You are a friend."

"Call me Arthur, please!"

"All right, Arthur it is."

He left, determined to help her leave that establishment, for he hated the thought of how she was used. He tried not to think of the men with whom she would have to be with tonight and every night. It made him angry.

He realised that he loved Caroline Davey.

WHERE WERE THE CHILDREN?

Caroline had come to know the other girls now. They were fifteen in number. She was astounded at how nice some of them were, how caring and sisterly they were to her. She had never thought that a fallen woman could reflect anything of God's goodness. But she was one of them now, she reminded herself, with a little humility. When people looked upon her, they would judge her unfairly.

Perhaps what had happened to her had happened to them.

But then she learned that some of them were there by their own free will. A few had been married and left their husbands and children. They were addicted to gin and could not bear to be sober.

Bess had come to the Lanyard via Mrs. Tait also. It was a comfort to know that somebody else had been through what she had endured. Bess had answered an advertisement for a housemaid, been met at the station, and taken to Palm Street 'to visit an old friend.' Her family never heard from her again, for she was too ashamed to write, even if she had pen and paper.

There were one or two whom Caroline avoided, for they were jealous of the younger women. She was in the bloom of youth and they were fading, their withering hurried by hard living, by gin and opium. Janey and Nell were sad, angry women. She wondered what would become of them when they became old. They'd have to chaperone the younger ones like Flossie and Elsie did now. Those last two were toothless, querulous, and Mrs. McDonald treated them very badly. They worked in the kitchen and only got scraps to eat.

"The only place they could go would be the workhouse," said Bess, "And they can't get gin there."

"I don't want to end up like that," said Caroline, shivering.

The first meal of the day at the Lanyard was at noon, which was a breakfast of porridge, dry bread, and tea. Caroline seated herself one day at the long table in the lounge bar where they ate, and as the communal bowl of porridge was brought to the table by Flossie, she felt a wave of nausea wash over her. She left the table and felt better after half an hour, and that evening ate her dinner, boiled sheeps trotters and watery vegetables, accompanied by stale bread rolls. They rarely saw good meat or fish.

The following day, the same thing happened at breakfast. Again, she left the table. At dinner time that evening, her sick stomach had settled.

By now, her morning discomfort had been noticed. The following morning, as the smell of porridge caused her to turn pale, Flossie laughed.

"Someone's got a bun in the oven," she said to nobody in particular.

"Shut up, Flossie. She doesn't know what that means," said Eppie, one of the kind women.

"She'll know soon enough," cackled old Flossie.

Some of the girls looked at her with sympathy. Caroline had no idea what they were talking about. Flossie went away, singing *"Rock a bye-baby, on a treetop, When the wind blows, the cradle will rock,"* in a crackly voice, infused with glee.

"Stop it, Flossie!" said Eppie, angrily.

Caroline was confused. What was going on? She fought the nausea, willing it to go away. But it wasn't working. She got up.

"She don't know nothin', does she?" said Janey with undisguised contempt, upon seeing the confusion on her face.

"If she'd grown up in one room with her mother and father and eight young brothers and sisters like I did, she'd know plenty," added Nell, with equal contempt.

"Have a heart," Eppie reprimanded them.

Their meaning began to dawn on Caroline. She felt stupid, not knowing. Sometime after little Archie was born, she'd asked Auntie Mary for a fuller explanation as to how babies came to be, but she had answered that there was no need for her to know any more until she had decided to marry. Now she understood.

Later in the day, as she put on rouge and carmine in preparation for the evening's business, she felt both frightened and excited.

Now they will let me go, she thought. *Because I won't be any good to them with a baby! They will have to let me go!*

I will tell people I'm a widow, and work hard for myself and the baby!

The door opened and Mrs. McDonald came in, a glass of dark liquid in her hand.

"I heard of your little indisposition," she said in a caring tone Caroline had never heard her use. "I got you some medicine."

"You know?"

"I know. And I'm giving you a few nights off, even more if you need. Drink this, I always gives it to my girls."

She took the large glass in her hand and sipped. It tasted horrid.

"Must I, Mrs. McDonald?"

"You must. I promise it will do you the greatest good in the world, it will."

She seemed almost motherly. Mrs. McDonald stood and watched her and Caroline was reminded strongly of the last time someone had made sure she had taken a drink. Were they about to kill her, because of the baby? She shoved the glass, half-emptied, back at Mrs. McDonald.

"I don't need it!" she cried.

"That's all right, dear. You've taken enough," Mrs. McDonald said smoothly. "Now I must ask you to go to the sick bay, top of the house. This room is only for business. Flossie will show you."

Flossie was outside the door and led the way upstairs. The sick bay was only a narrow bed in her and Elsie's dirty room in the attic, stuffed into a dusty corner under the sloping ceiling, with an excuse for a curtain drawn about it. The bed had discoloured old sheets, patched over and over.

By now, Caroline was very uneasy. She put her nightdress on and lay down. She felt very tired and drifted to sleep. It occurred to her that none of the women had children, but they must have conceived as she did. *Where were the children?*

She dreamed she was on a riverbank, and saw a small child in the water, being taken downstream in a strong, rapid current. She plunged in, wading as fast as she could, but the child disappeared in the flow. She grieved, crying out.

She awoke, gripped by intense pain. A thousand claws were tearing her insides to pieces.

DEATH BECKONS

Caroline felt she was near death. She knew what had happened, and what the 'medicine' had been for. It had been to rid her of the child. Such a thing had never even occurred to her when she had taken it. What a wicked world it was!

She didn't care if she died.

The pains had abated somewhat, but she was too weak to even move her limbs. She was conscious of people bending over her. One was Mrs. McDonald, the other was Mrs. Tait, and another was Hippo, one of Mrs. McDonald's several Bullies who kept the girls and the men in order.

"Hippo, I don't want 'er to die 'ere in this house," snapped Mrs. McDonald. "Go get a cart, cover it with tarpaulin, and tek her out to Hampstead."

"To Mrs. Madders?"

"Yes, who else lives in Hampstead? If she dies there, Beryl can bury 'er, out there where there aren't any nosey neighbours. Here's a pound to give her."

Now Eppie's face came into view, contorted with worry.

"We should get a doctor," she said, desperately.

"You fool! He'd know what I done."

"You could have killed her, Meg. I told you that stuff was strong. If she had taken the whole lot, we'd be looking at a corpse."

"I don't want no corpse here in this house. Come on, help me, get her off the bed with me."

BAWD'S DAUGHTER

Caroline did not know where she was, except that she was outside the city in a small cottage with a smell of smoke and a kettle singing on the fire. She awoke to see a young woman shelling peas, seated on a stool by the fire.

"Oh good, you're awake. Ma sent you here to die, but I thought you might live. I got the doctor for you."

She was still alive. The realisation disappointed her.

"What's wrong with you? You don't want to live, is that it?"

"Your mother is Mrs. McDonald?"

"Yes, that's me Ma. That's not her real name, though. Nasty one, isn't she?"

Caroline was very surprised.

"Me Pa tried to take me away from 'er. He was a good bloke, was me Pa. But she found me an' took me back, an' same thing as I know 'appened to you, 'appened to me. Only I was much younger."

"Good grief!" Caroline struggled to sit up, astonished. "What a horrible woman!"

"Yeah, she is. It's the gin and the poker. She 'as to 'ave money for the gin and poker. My husband can't stand 'er. He's out getting coal. It's cold today, isn't it?" She took up the poker and shook up the coals in the fire.

Could she trust this woman, this daughter of Mrs. McDonald, and niece of Mrs. Tait, who said her own mother was bad? She decided that she could trust nobody. She never would trust anybody again.

"Here's my plan. I'll tell me Ma you died, and you can go 'ome."

"They don't want me at home."

"Well, go somewheres else then. Unless you want to go back to me Ma."

"Oh no, that's the last thing I want to do."

"I'm Mrs. Madders. Call me Beryl."

"I'm Caroline," she said it very deliberately. "Caroline Mary Davey."

"There's this Christian woman, then. Her name is Mrs. May. She lives here in Hampstead. She it was got me a job 'ere, then I got married. She'll take you in and train you in a trade. I'll give you her address."

"Christian? Will I have to attend services, then? Because I don't believe in God anymore. He didn't help me when I needed it."

"He's helping you now, in't he? Or do you not want the help?"

Caroline considered this. God's help coming from a member of the bawd's family was an unexpected source, but she could not deny that it was help.

"You can 'ave her address. Ma will think you died, she was expecting you to die anyhow. She was terrified she'd hang. I'll make you some beef tea. The doctor says you're undernourished."

"All right then," Caroline said. She sank back on her pillow. She was going to be free at last, but she felt as helpless as a newborn kitten.

WHERE IS CARO?

"Have I got bad news for you," said Mrs. McDonald when she next saw Arthur come in. "Your favourite is not here anymore, sorry to say."

Arthur's surprise was genuine. *That was quick,* he said to himself. *She's taken my advice and escaped!* He felt deflated that he had not had the opportunity to bid her goodbye. He supposed that she had seen an opportunity and taken it. Why should she have stayed one minute longer than necessary? But where did she go?

"She's not here? I have to say I am surprised, because we had our usual Friday appointment."

"There won't be any more of those. But,there are these other girls."

Arthur shook his head.

"I suppose you can't tell me where she's gone," he asked nonchalantly. It would be odd if he had no curiosity.

"Heaven or Hell," was the reply from Mrs. McDonald. "Where else is there, when you die? I'll be off to Hell, myself."

"Die?" Arthur felt his head spin. Was he really hearing this?

"Yes, she took sick and I sent her out the country for a cure, but I got word this morning that she died."

"Where did you send her?"

"Out the country, I told you."

She's gotten rid of Caro, sent her to another house, and she doesn't want me looking for her. She thinks I got too attached to her.

"I don't believe you," he accused her.

"Well, you better believe me." She thrust a hand into her pocket and drew out a letter. It was written in a rough, female hand.

Dear Ma, regret to inform you Lilya died yesterday. Burial here tomorrow at Hampstead. Beryl.

It hit him like a brick. He could not believe that Caroline was dead, and yet, here it was. He turned and stumbled away to the door.

"I do hate it when they get attached," said Mrs. McDonald crossly. "Nobody else will do fer 'em then, and we lose 'em."

ARTHUR IN HAMPSTEAD

Hampstead was a large area with a growing population, and Arthur did not know where to begin. Part of it was urban and part was rural. He could go to the churches there and make enquiries about burials He wondered what name would have been given for her, Lilya something, or Caroline Davey?

But no church, not St. Johns-at-Hampstead nor any other, could help him. There were no funeral arrangements for a young woman as described who had lost her life in the last few days. Such a person would be notable for having no relatives. A woman had died in childbirth on Wednesday, but there was a heartbroken husband and a large family of mourners.

Arthur concluded his search, convinced that she was alive. He was very hopeful. Caroline must have employed some subterfuge to feign illness and be sent away and accomplished her escape. It did not explain the note, but perhaps she had known Mrs. McDonald's daughter and taken her into her confidence. He admired her for it, even though he had lost her, perhaps forever.

I must stop thinking about Caroline, he said to himself as he sat on a bench and munched an apple. The fruit was his main source of sustenance these days. Bread and cheese, supplemented by apples, was his usual daily fare if he did not work. He was hungry most of the day and tried to postpone his first meal until he could bear the hunger no longer. He bought day-old bread from bakeries at half-price as they were about to close their doors. He drank from standpipes and slept in parks and doorways.

I must find regular work, he thought. He pulled out a sheet of paper from his inside pocket and unfolded it carefully. It was a character that Father Abbot had given him. Not many men had a reference from a monastery, and he wondered who would be most impressed by it.

It was time to get on with his life.

MRS. MAY

Caroline was so afraid that Mrs. McDonald would visit her daughter to see for herself whether she was alive or dead, that she dragged herself out of bed and left the cottage that very day. Mrs. May's home was not a long walk, but it exhausted her, and as she peered through the iron gate, she wondered if she would be able to get as far as the door.

It was a large old house that brought back memories of Uncle Edward. She found that comforting. How she had been afraid of that house as a child! Yet she had learned that buildings do not matter as much as the hearts of those who live in them. She pushed the heavy gate inand walked slowly up the path. She ought to go around to the back door, of course, but she did not think she would last that long before having to sit down.

Her arrival had been noted by someone inside, for a man and a woman came out. It was Mrs. May and her butler. They helped her the rest of the way.

A neat room in the servant's quarters was prepared for her, and there she slept for the remainder of the evening, a bright fire burning in the grate. Toward nightfall she took a little nourishment and slept very well. The servant who attended her was friendly and chatty.

Mrs. May visited her the next day and heard her story.

"My dear," she said, patting her hand. "We must let your family know you are alive."

She shook her head.

"I prefer them to think me dead, Mrs. May. I'm ruined. I bring no disgrace if I'm dead. My turning up would cause gossip and speculation, and bring a shadow over my uncle's ministry. Please do not ask me to contact them."

"Very well, dear. I shall not do so. However, when you feel better, we should go to the police."

"Oh no, ma'am, I could not. Really, I could not."

"Very well, we will not talk of it, but consider this. These wicked women are luring other innocent girls into prostitution and will continue until they are stopped. Think about that, and when you are ready, let me know. The police may well be able to keep your name out of it, and carry out independent inquiries. I shall not mention it again, for I know it distresses you. Now, may I pray with you?"

"But is not God angry with me?"

"Angry with you, Caroline! Why would He be angry with you?"

She told her about Horace.

"And you think God punished you for that. Goodness, child. You don't know our Saviour. I think perhaps, though, that when we sin, we weaken God's protection over us, but I'm no learned theologian or Scripture scholar. Now may I pray with you?"

Caroline nodded.

Mrs. May prayed the Lord's Prayer, and Caroline found herself joining in. She then prayed 'The Lord is my Shepherd,' and Caroline found that the words reached her soul in a way that they had never done before.

Walk in the valley of the shadow of Death. Surely she had been there! She knew what it was to walk in the valley of the shadow of death! The psalm seemed to speak to her soul, as if the psalmist had written it just for her. She wanted to sob, and when Mrs. May had left the room, she did, into her pillow, for some time.

During her recovery, she had a great deal of time to think and to pray. Her mother had told her that sorrow was *'going through life.'* Some people had more than others. Some people led charmed lives. Some, like her, had loss after loss, sorrow after sorrow. What was the meaning of it? How could a person go through life without being hurt or scarred?

POLICE

C aroline recovered her physical strength quickly. Emotionally, however, she was mending very slowly. She felt relieved and almost happy one day, only to find that the next brought her misery and wretchedness of spirit. So much sorrow, pain, and loss had visited her in such a short time, that she wondered if happiness was ever possible again.

"I think we'll move you to Whitechapel soon," Mrs. May said cheerfully one morning.

"The hostel, you mean?"

"Bethany Lodging for Women. You need the company of other girls. There are ten girls there as we speak. Three are training as milliners, one is a seamstress, and others have not decided."

"All rescued by you, Mrs. May, from different brothels."

Mrs. May nodded.

"I have been thinking on what you said, about going to the police," Caroline said. "I would like those women to be stopped from harming other girls. And those who are in Palm Street and Lanyard, could be freed, could they not?"

"Yes, my dear. Those who remained of their own accord might face some trouble, and the old ones you told me about, the workhouse will be the only place for them. It's unfortunate that anybody should end their days there." Mrs. May pressed her hand. "You are taking the correct path, Caroline, though I know it is hard for you. I have a policeman friend, an Inspector Lightfoot, who I frequently call upon in matters of this sort. I shall send a message for him to visit and you may give him the particulars."

The following morning, which was Saturday, Inspector Lightfoot and a young constable were in the drawing room at eleven o' clock sharp, and Caroline, hesitant at first from the natural shame of what had happened to her, soon warmed and gave them a full statement of what had happened to her. Mrs. May's presence was an encouragement. The

Inspector and the constable showed the essence of kindness and gravity. When she disclosed that a policeman on the beat was a regular visitor and kept Mrs. Tait out of trouble, the Inspector's countenance grew rock-hard.

"He visits there every Saturday," added Caroline.

The Inspector told the constable to make a note of it.

"There may well be another poor girl in Palm Street now," said Caroline. "I cannot bear to think of it. Am I, will I have to, appear in court?"

"We may not need you to do so. Luring somebody on the pretext of giving them a position may be easier to prosecute, since there may be letters to attest to that fact, and fathers and mothers to say they too saw and read those letters, and so on."

Caroline was very relieved.

ARREST

A t eleven o'clock that night, Mrs. Tait, downing her fourth gin of the evening, was aghast to hear the loud knock on the door, and the shout of "POLICE! OPEN UP!"

There was nothing she could do. Her policeman friend was upstairs with the girl who had arrived three days ago from Hampshire. No time to even warn him, and several minutes later he was dragged downstairs, his uniform buttoned the wrong way, his eyes bulging in his head, and trying to tell them that they were completely misunderstanding the situation.

The Hampshire girl was rescued by a police matron, Mrs. Albertson. "Give her back her own clothes," she ordered Mrs. Tait, who meekly obeyed. She was trembling with terror as she handed over the cheap but beautifully sewn garments to the matron. She had this time posed as the manager of a posh dressmaker's in Mayfair, and had to divert, of course, to Palm Street on the way there, to visit a retired seamstress whose beautiful work she wished her to admire.

Mrs. Tait was then handcuffed and marched away. She had no way to warn her sister.

At the Lanyard Arms, the evening was in full swing, and Mrs. McDonald was playing a game of poker in the back room when the raid came. She was swiftly arrested, but protested strongly that she was only running a music-hall and that everything was very respectable. The men had stampeded out the back-door as soon as they got a chance. They practically climbed over each other to get away lest their names appear in the paper.

65
CAB STAND

Arthur had acquired a steady job driving a hackney cab. As he drove about the streets of the East End, his eyes never failed to scan the faces of the female figures he saw on the pathways or crossing in front of him. There was one he longed to see was Caroline. The other he wished to see was his sister Eleanor. Were both lost forever?

He supposed that Caro had forgotten him. She was young and now had her own life to lead. He hoped that she had gone into service in a good house or even returned to her home in Cheapside. As for Eleanor, she could be living in squalor, or even dead from some dreadful disease. He still could not understand how she had done what she did, but she had hurt herself most of all. He wished to know if she was well, at least. His mother grieved for her in every letter and asked if he had heard anything of her. He heard nothing at all from Matthew, and Gregory's whereabouts were unknown.

His needs were little, and the other drivers teased him about his bachelor life and his sober habits. They knew nothing of his past, but some had got wind that his character had come from an Abbot, so they called him 'the monk,' a nickname he hardly liked, but he had to concede that it was in keeping with his quiet, frugal lifestyle. He was trying to save as much as he could.

One day, he was at his usual stand, near Euston Station, and he was polishing the brass fittings of his cab when the other drivers, most engaged in their own little maintenance jobs between fares, began to talk.

"Jem? Did you 'ear of those wicked sisters?" George was giving his horse a drink from a pail.

"I did! I never 'eard such a wicked thing done as what they did. It should be a 'angin' offense, that."

"The law 'as gone soft, it 'as." Chuggy, so named because he liked to 'chug along' as he said, was scraping some dried mud from the spokes of his wheels. "An' I bet they'll be transported. Wait till you

274

see. A nice sea voyage out to a land that gets more sunshine than England, tha's what I've 'eard, an' they get rich after. Crime pays."

Arthur smiled grimly and rubbed the brass a little harder.

"My missus is furious they're not being tried for murder, for she says those girls are as good as dead. She says it could 'ave been our Cassie or Tess that was trapped by those women. There's nothing she'd like better than to go an' see 'em swing at Newgate," Jem said then.

"You know what I think, Jem? Those parents that let their daughters come 'ere, to the big city, on their own, them as should be taken out an' shot. There's no end of girls that 'ave disappeared, they'll never be able to count 'em. I bet some of 'em are dead."

"What is this? Who are these women on trial?" Arthur asked, looking up.

"You don't know? It's a trial at the Old Bailey. You need to get out more, Monk. These wicked sisters, bawds they were, advertised in newspapers posing as housekeepers for good houses, and promised jobs."

"Where did they operate?"

"One of 'em had a place in Gullseye, near the dockyards. The other I don't rightly know."

This was a revelation indeed! He could not get his thoughts from the affair, and the following day he took some time off to attend the trial. There, in the packed courtroom, straight ahead of him in the dock, stood Mrs. McDonald and the other woman, the one who had kidnapped Caroline, Mrs. Tait. Mrs. McDonald did not look so brash now. There was no smirk on her face. Mrs. Tait looked thoroughly frightened. Arthur looked around for Caroline, but could not see her. After that, he followed the case in the Daily Telegraph.

JUSTICE IS SERVED

Many girls came forward to give evidence, and as the Inspector predicted, produced letters and witnesses. Reporters wrote on the case, and it was news in every part of the country. Hopeful parents and friends of girls who had disappeared in London waited for news of their loved one, a letter, a note, but most were disappointed. Only a few parents had good news. None of the girls returned home. They would be known for life as the girls who were ruined by the Wicked Women of Gullseye, as the Press dubbed them. The girls would make better lives for themselves where they could begin afresh. Mrs. May's lodging house was full now.

The Jury found Mrs. Tait (Roberts) and Mrs. McDonald (Walters), for they had operated under false names, guilty of several crimes. They were to be imprisoned for the remainder of their natural lives. A few days before they sailed, Mrs. Walters died of a heart attack at Newgate Prison. Mrs. Roberts would not even have the comfort of her sister as she faced living out her days in a strange, spartan land, which she thought of as foreign as the moon. She considered her sister luckier than she was. She left England a very different woman from the Mrs. Tait of Palm Street, as silent and as terrified as she had rendered her young victims, and constantly on the watch against attacks and thefts of the necessities of life by the younger, stronger prisoners.

T HE GOOD DEED

Caroline let herself in to the little shop that was hers to run, just two rooms, a front to serve customers, and a back to conduct the shop's business and to store the merchandise. It was a wet day in May. She pulled up the shutters, humming to herself, and light flooded the shop. The carefully arranged display of hats, big and showy, little and sweet, with high feathers and draping ribbons and elegant bows, delighted her as it always did.

Which of these beauties for the window today, she wondered. Colourful, light, and summery hats, they seemed to invite themselves to sit in the window to be admired by passersby. She chose a blue velvet toque trimmed with white braid and a high ostrich feather.

The shop was in one of the streets leading off Whitechapel. Caroline liked her work. She spent her day making and trimming hats and dealing with customers. There were not that many, for there was competition on the High Street itself, but it was adequate.

She had, in the years since she had escaped, never allowed a man to court her, though there were plenty willing, even some who knew what she had been. She was twenty-three now and did not think she would ever get married. She was happy on her own. She tried not to think too much about the 'missing years,' as she termed them to herself. They were a series of nightmares, now passed. Her life had altered forever, but she had tried to make her peace with it as it was now. She was poor, just getting by, one of many needing the funds collected regularly from Mrs. May's charitable donors in the more fashionable areas of London. The shop did not make very much but she was respectable again, at least in her own eyes, and there was nobody about to point fingers at her.

The shop was not hers, but it was hers to run, indefinitely. In the years since she had lodged at

Bethany House, she had gained seniority, and Mrs. May and the other girls trusted her. She wondered sometimes what it would be like to have a home of her own, with a hearth and children gathering about her. A home was a normal and natural thing for a young woman to wish for. But she was not normal, not now, not anymore.

She brought supplies from the back to the front room and began to cut ribbon to make trimming for the straw hats that were popular in summer. She saw a woman at the window, one of those truly unfortunate women who, unlike herself, became addicted to gin and sold themselves night after night for a few bottles to get them through the next day. She knew this woman by sight. She had been pretty once, but now her skin was bad and her eyes hollow in her head. Fair wispy hair strayed from under an old straw bonnet.

Caroline got to her feet and opened the door.

"What's the matter?" she asked, as the woman fell against the window, clutching her stomach as if in agony. A policeman was called, who called a doctor, who said that she would have to be removed to Hospital.

"I'm going to die," muttered the woman, tears in her eyes.

"Do you have anybody I can call to help you?" asked Caroline. She often saw herself in those older women, if she had not escaped and made her way to Mrs. May. Not that she was that old, probably not even thirty-five.

The woman burst into sobbing. The policeman carried her to the ambulance van. Caroline returned to her work, but she had no peace.

"I will have to go and see her," she said to the girls that evening as they were gathered in their living room, a simple but cosy common room where they ate and chatted, washed out their clothes, did necessary mending, and read fashion magazines. They were not allowed to drink alcohol there, but some girls, who had not yet managed to break the habit, went out at night.

"If you get involved in somebody's life, it can be very complicated," warned Bess.

"I know, but I just can't leave her like that. She's alone. She might wish to reform her life and come here."

"Oh Miss Davey, do you think the likes of us will ever own a gown like that?" asked Trudy, a girl of seventeen, turning over the pages of *The Englishwoman's Domestic Magazine.* "White swiss muslin, and six flounces!"

Caroline smiled fondly at her. It was hard to believe that only a few weeks ago, this girl had been in the greatest misery. "Work hard, stay sober, and believe in God's goodness, even when things look dark. Maybe your happiness won't lie in having beautiful gowns, but you will find peace and contentment. And keep learning! Don't just stay with the fashion plates. Read the articles on cookery, budgeting, and housekeeping also," she added.

"Oh, yes, Miss Davey," said the girl.

An hour later, she was at St. Thomas' Hospital, inquiring for the woman who had been picked up in Gullseye that morning. The porter was helpful, and soon she was staring at the woman whose name she had been told was 'Mrs. Smith,' lying flat on a bed in the ward. She had a white nightgown and cap, and was awake.

"Do you remember me from this morning?" Caroline asked kindly, sat on the bed.

The woman nodded.

"My name is Caroline Davey. You were afraid you were dying, now you see, you are getting better," she added in a bright tone.

The woman managed a little smile of gratitude at her caring tone.

"Thank you, but in truth, I'd rather be dead."

"Please don't say that! I was once as you were, but I now have a little shop, not mine really, but it makes me happy with myself."

"You did not do what I did. I have to tell somebody, before I die, what I did."

"If it eases you, you may tell me, and I will listen, and then I will forget all. And nobody is saying you will die, except you, for I spoke to the nurse on my way in."

Caroline patted her hand.

"I grew up in a country parsonage," the woman began.

This was surprising indeed!

"My father had a living in Nottinghamshire, on the estate of a man named Harries. Our life was good. Very good."

"Go on," Caroline encouraged her gently as she hesitated.

"I fell in love with the eldest Harries son, a boy named Gregory. But he did not love me in return!"

Caroline patted her hand.

"It's a common enough situation, unfortunately," she said. "Many women give their love to men who are undeserving of it. And I suppose the reverse is true too."

Thank Heaven I am finished with men forever, she thought to herself.

"I had a wonderful sister, and a little brother. Our parents were good people! Our life was good. But I repeat myself."

After another little pause she went on.

"An old man in the village was assaulted and robbed one night. Gregory placed the blame on my little brother, and he was sent down for seven long years."

Something began to stir in Caroline's memory.

"And I, God forgive me! I then betrayed my own family by consenting to run away with Gregory Harries!"

"He asked you to marry him then?"

"Yes, two days before we were to leave for Ireland, for my father lost the living, you know. The people turned against us. The mob turned out. That hurt him. Gregory came to me when I was in the orchard looking at everything for the last time and asked me to marry him. Miss Caroline, all my dreams came true in that moment when he drew me to him and told me that he loved me! But I was very, very mistaken. I should have known, when he told me it would have to be an elopement. But I was blindly in love!

"He lied when he said he loved me. I found out later that he thought that if he got married, his father would stop nagging him. They knew it was he, you see, who robbed Mr. Leamy. And they were very angry with him for it, but would not allow the family to know disgrace and ruin among all their friends, so they colluded to blame my brother. Then Gregory, selfish as always, thought that if he got married, his father would think him serious about repenting his wild ways and also give him some of his inheritance. And I was the only girl he knew who would consent to be swept off my feet in an elopement. In other words, I was the only fool he knew.

"But they did not react the way he thought they would. He wrote to them from Nottingham, where we stayed a week together in an Inn, to say he was getting married directly. They wrote back and said that if he married *me*, they would disinherit him! They wanted no connection between our families. Gregory abandoned me there and then. From there, I came here."

It was a horrid little story. Nottingham. Seven years. Caroline remembered something very vaguely from some years ago, from Arthur Ellis. Arthur Ellis! She had not thought of him in months now, but every time something reminded her of him, his name brought forth a warm feeling of gratitude and respect, and she saw again in her mind his calm blue-grey eyes and how he spoke in a measured, wise way.

"Was he imprisoned? Your brother?"

"He was sentenced to prison. I have not heard of him since, nor of my family. They would not wish to know me in any case. How stupid I was! I often wonder if it was idolatry. I loved Gregory Harries more than I loved God. See where it got me!"

Caroline smiled gently.

"Please don't worry. I think I have met your brother. Is it Arthur?"

This caused a glow of hope to come over the woman's face.

"Did he return, then? Is he safe?"

"I have not seen him for many years now. But yes, he returned. He helped me greatly, for I was in the deepest distress at the time. I was only a girl and he was truly kind to me, but it is a long, long story, Miss Ellis. He was healthy, and was determined to make something of himself. He did go to Nottingham, I remember. But what for exactly, I do not recall."

"It eases me greatly to know that. I wrote several times to my family in Ireland, via the Parsonage at Middledene, but if the letters were ever forwarded, they have not written back. I am dead to them."

"When the hospital discharges you, Miss Ellis, will you come to us, at Bethany? You can make a fresh start. And I'm going to try to find Arthur to tell him you are alive and well."

"Oh, to see my little brother! Or any of my family again!" Eleanor began to weep.

68

REUNION

Caroline had no idea where to find Mr. Ellis. She racked her brains to remember all he had said about himself, but most of their conversations had been about her. There must be a way to find him, if he was still in London! It would be a good way to repay him for his kindness to her.

Then it occurred to her that she could put an advertisement in the paper. She wrote it out carefully, giving a box number for a reply.

If Mr. Arthur Ellis, formerly of Nottinghamshire reads this, or comes to know of this advertisement, there is a message awaiting him at PO Box 117, in this newspaper office.

It was clumsily put, she thought, but it was best not to go into detail. She walked to the Morning News office in Lombard Street, and the Daily Telegraph in Fleet Street. She hoped he would read one of them. She could not afford to place it in any more than two.

Arthur had, since the trial, bought a daily newspaper to keep up with the world. He was startled to see his own name staring him in the face one day from the Morning News. What could this be? Was it Matthew Harries, about to confess and clear him? Would he at last get a pardon?

He set off at a smart pace to Fleet Street. He asked the clerk if he could remember who had handed in the notice.

"A nice young lady, I remember," said the clerk. "Not very tall, but comely, dark-eyed, a very nice young lady."

Not Matthew then. Who could it be? He opened the message in the box, and his heart leaped.

Dear Mr. Ellis, You will not have heard anything of me for a long time, nor I of you. I hope you are well. I have come into some knowledge that will be of great interest to you. I live at Bethany Lodging for Women, Pearl Lane, Whitechapel.

There may be a surprise awaiting you there, if you do not delay.

Yours sincerely,

Caroline Davey.

He knew all along that she was alive! Still, the confirmation of it was very welcome.

It was not his pardon, nor even the promise of it. But renewing his friendship with Caroline would equal it in happiness. What could she be talking of? He would go there tonight, as soon as he finished his shift at eight.

69

BROTHER AND SISTER

He knocked on the door of the house in the quiet lane that evening shortly after eight, and a servant answered. He was shown into a parlour, there to await Miss Davey, who the girl said would be fetched immediately.

He sat on the edge of the chair, his hat in his hand, nervous. What was she like now? What was *he* like now? He had improved in looks, he thought. Years of regular food had restored him to full health and energy. But did he look older? Would she think him old? He was thirty now.

He jumped to his feet as the door opened.

She was there before him. Taller than he remembered, her figure more mature, her eyes lit up, clear and smiling. She had bloomed into a beautiful woman. Her dress was modest and charming. He felt tongue-tied, awkward, face to face with the girl who had captured his heart.

"Arthur!" She came toward him with hands outstretched to take his. "You have not changed one iota. You're still the same as you were! It is good to see you again!"

"And you, Miss Davey, Caroline." He could hardly speak for happiness at the warm greeting. "You look so happy.".

"And I am, Arthur, as much as I can be." she spoke softly, and drew him down on the sofa, where she seated herself. "You must have heard about the wicked sisters. I was freed before that."

"Mrs. McDonald told me you were dead, but I did not believe her."

"She thought I was dead. I became very ill and near death."

Caroline suddenly had a resurgence of memories at the harrowing time, how she had felt like a small animal in a trap. Why did past events have the power to flood the mind with fresh pain? She let go of his hands and stood, walking toward the window.

"I am sorry," he said quickly.

"No, do not be. You were so good to help me. You understood in a way nobody else did."

Now it was his turn to be stabbed with memories so painful that he had covered it for many years. He got to his feet and twisted his hat in his hands.

"We both suffered. Miss Davey, you said in your note."

"No, allow me to tell you what happened. First, she made me ill. I was with child, and she made me lose it. I was near death, and she sent me to her daughter in Hampstead, who had suffered also at her hands, and who told me to contact Mrs. May, a good Christian woman. She owns this house. Mrs. Madders told her mother I had died, and I was happy to have Mrs. McDonald, or Walters as she was, believe that. But how have you been, Mr. Ellis? No, I shall not call you Mr. Ellis. I will always call you Arthur. What are you doing now?"

He began to tell her, but before he had reached Sherwood Monastery, she cut him short.

"You must tell me another time, Arthur, for I cannot keep your surprise from you any longer. I must prepare you, first. It is someone you have not seen in a very long time. She is unsure as to how you will receive her."

"Eleanor! Not my sister Eleanor! Is it?" his eyes were alight with happiness.

"Oh, yes, it is! And you will forgive her, Arthur, won't you? She is so sorry and has suffered so much! She is making a very big effort to reform her life."

"Of course I will forgive her."

Caroline ran outside, called excitedly downstairs, and having witnessed the happy and very tearful reunion, left the brother and sister to themselves and sent up tea.

LOVE BECKONS

A very happy time followed this reunion. Arthur called often on Sundays to take the girls out. He walked in the park with his sister on one arm and the woman he loved on the other, and hoped that in time, they would call each other sister. He had been saving hard and would soon be in a position to settle down, in a modest flat in a respectable area. Would Caroline marry him? He was not sure. She showed no sign of being in love with him, though she thought him a dear friend.

One day, he confided his hopes to Eleanor.

"Has she ever said `anything of me that would lead you to believe that she likes me, that I might be a favourite?"

"Oh little brother! I don't know. But I have heard her say she doesn't know if she will marry. She said she might marry for children, though."

"That is disappointing. She does not intend to fall in love, then."

"What will become of me, Arthur?" Eleanor asked suddenly. "I am a burden to everybody. I have no trade, no skill. I cannot go as a governess, or a companion, or anything."

"I don't know. Does not Mrs. May have placements for women?"

"Yes, but I am older than they. I could get married, you know. There is a man who I lived with for some time. He wishes to marry me."

"Do you love him?"

"I don't believe in love. Look where it got me! And, he drinks."

"Don't marry without love, Eleanor." He remembered something. "When I met Matthew Harries, he told me that he had offered to marry you. Was that true?"

"Yes, he did. It was gallant of him. And he liked me a little, I think. But I refused. If Gregory returned, how awkward all that would be, should we meet for family occasions and suchlike. No, it would be impossible."

"What did Gregory do with all that money of Mr. Leamy's?"

"I do not know, but it would not last him forever. It was a great fortune to a poor man, but no Harries could live on that amount for six months."

Caroline knew that Arthur was in love with her. It troubled her, for she did not wish to hurt him, and yet she did not want to be in love with him, or anybody. But sometimes Eleanor fell back to admire a shrub or a flower and she found herself walking alone with him. She knew why Eleanor was doing this, and it troubled her. Not that she did not like having Arthur to herself. He was the only person in the world to whom she could speak freely about anything. The girls were wonderful company, and they were all very solicitous of each other, but as she was in charge at Bethany, there was a little distance between them, a little deference. As well as that most of their childhoods had been very different from hers. Many were tradesmen's daughters and had not known plenty of anything, and none had ever had a governess. Some had been raised in abject poverty and need, knowing constant hunger and cold. A few had been servants that had gone wrong and then been abandoned. Her past was a mystery to them, for she could not divulge anything about it to them. All they knew was that she had an uncle who was a clergyman, and that, in itself, was very exalted to most.

She and Arthur had similar backgrounds and no explanations were necessary when they chatted. And he knew her secret, her shame. Her inner heart was known to him. She sometimes felt that she had known him all of her life. His features were dear to her, too. He was handsome in a way, though when she remembered Horace Watts, a man she remembered with a glow sometimes, he was not at all as handsome as Mr. Watts. Her lost love! Did he miss her for very long, she wondered. Sometimes she found herself looking at any gentleman who passed by, just in case it was Mr. Watts. But he was about twenty-five now, and married, perhaps.

"I can't stay silent any longer, Caro," Arthur said quietly one day. "You must know that I love you,"

She did not reply.

"Oh no, I have spoiled it now. We have a great friendship, don't we? And now I've ruined it, haven't I?"

"No, Arthur, you haven't ruined it. I always want to be your friend! Always!"

"Only that? Only my friend?"

"I wish to stay as I am."

"And I do not, Caroline. But I know I should not have spoken. If you can't think of me, we should not see so much of each other."

I've hurt him. Caroline thought. But there was little else to be said.

"I appreciate your candour," he said then. He turned and called to Eleanor, who had lagged behind for an hour now, reading a book as she walked along the path behind them.

C aroline felt a shadow over the next few days. She did not want to hurt Arthur, and it distressed her to do so. But she did not feel anything of a quickening pulse when he was near, or any flutter in her heart when he was close to her. It made her gloomy.

Sunday came, and Arthur did not come. Eleanor proposed they walk out on their own, and Caroline accompanied her to the park, but Arthur was not there.

After that, Arthur called to see Eleanor and took her out for a walk, but Caroline was not one of the party. She felt aggrieved. When would she hear that there was a girl he admired, to whom he was paying court? Would she become jealous?

But she had little time to ponder, for something else occurred to occupy her mind. She was walking one day along a busy street, with costermongers and sellers crying out, when she beheld an old woman fall not ten paces away. She rushed to her aid, together with some other people, including a young girl aged about seventeen. They got the woman to her feet and handed her over to the care of her daughter who was nearby. Eleanor turned about to see that the girl who had helped her, a potato seller, had had her basket of meagre goods stolen and was now seated on a doorstep sobbing, her head against the railing.

"It's no good," she sobbed. "I can't do anything here, I can't keep myself, nor my sister! I don't know what to do now, for I have tried everything!"

Caroline recognised the accent, distinctly Devonshire! She sat beside her immediately to console her.

"Where are you from in Devonshire?" she asked, to make her feel easy.

The girl looked up suddenly, her eyes teary.

"Do you know Devonshire, then?"

"Of course! I'm from there," answered Caroline.

The girl cried again, with happiness this time.

"I'm from Fernleigh originally, which is a little village near Johns Mills," Caroline continued.

"But that's where I am from! Johns Mills!" cried the girl. "I and my sister lived with our grandmother in Fernleigh, name of Glennon, but she died and I brought my sister here."

"I am Davey. Caroline Davey. I have heard the name Glennon. IS there not a Doctor Glennon? He attended my dear mother, a long time ago."

"My father! And I have heard the name Davey," mused the girl. "I am Clare Glennon."

"Come with me back to my lodging," urged Miss Davey. "It's not far, and I'm sure you'd like a cup of tea."

"Thank you, but I can't. I have to get back to my sister. She is a simpleton, poor girl, and I don't like to leave her for long. She hates being left alone."

"If you do not live faraway, then we can call for her. How came you to be in London?"

Clare sighed. "It's a long story, our mother died. Our father remarried, but our new stepmother did not want Anna. Our father changed, especially when our stepmother gave him two sons, and so here we are, alone."

"It is a sad story, but all too common."

"My grandmother was against the marriage. She thought that Papa was acting too hastily after the loss of our mother. She didn't like the Sheltons. That is my stepmother's maiden name."

"Sheltons!" cried Miss Davey, stopping short in amazement.

"Yes, are you acquainted with them?"

"Yes, I am. They are relatives. No, don't be upset you mentioned them. Your grandmother was correct to mistrust them. I and my brother have been greatly injured by the Shelton family."

"My father married Henrietta Shelton," said Clare. "She was very unkind to my poor sister."

After that, the girls were instant friends. Miss Glennon had fled Fernleigh with her sister, a simple-minded girl, to avoid their father and stepmother sending her to the asylum. Miss Glennon soon introduced Anna, a smiling, childlike girl of twelve, who instantly showed Caroline the lace roses she was crocheting. "For hats," she said proudly.

"I make hats!" Caroline said warmly.

They lived in a cramped little room, most unsanitary, Caroline thought. She invited them to live with her at Bethany for a time, until times got better. She was afraid for them, and for their safety on the London streets.

Clare and Anna moved into Bethany. Clare helped in the kitchen, and Caroline brought Anna to work with her every day, where she sat and crocheted lace roses for the hats Caroline made. She loved her company, and Clare was very grateful for her help.

Miss Glennon soon realised that Bethany Lodging was a place for fallen women, and it was necessary for Caroline to give her its particular history, and hers, which she never liked to recall, but Clare was now a friend, and she too had seen the ugly side of human nature. She was horrified.

"You should write to your family, "she urged. "How dreadful for them, never to know what happened to you!"

"I fear it will be too late, and too much of a shock now," Caroline hedged.

"Would you really want your dear aunt to die not knowing what became of you, Miss Davey?"

73
GOING HOME

Clare's words made Caroline think more, and in the end, she decided that she would write a letter to the parsonage at St. Saviour's. She crafted it carefully.

Dear Aunt Mary,

You will be surprised to hear from me, after all these years. I am alive and well. The reason I could not write to tell you that is because after what happened to me, I thought it would be better if you all thought me dead. There, I have said it. To go back many years, I became lost in Surrey Gardens that evening, and having approached a seemingly-harmless older woman for assistance, found myself a prisoner in her home. What every young unmarried woman holds so precious was taken from me by force. I shall not tell you more. It would be distressing for us both, but only to mention that you may have heard of the trial of the Wicked Women of Gullseye some years ago. I was one of their victims.

For the last several years, I have been under the shelter of a most kind woman, Mrs. May, in whose lodging I live, as you see from the address above, in Whitechapel. I have a millinery shop which I run for her. I live a good life and am in charge of the Lodging.

I hope my Uncle is well. And my beloved brother Percy! How often I have thought of you all, and pined and grieved, especially in the first dreadful days and weeks. But I cannot speak of that. That is over. I have often wondered how the children are, and if there are any more Bartons.

Please do not be harsh with me for not contacting you.

She sealed the letter, addressed it to her aunt at St. Saviour's Church at Cheapside, and waited on tenterhooks for a day and a half. But no letter came. She had not written by return then. It was not a good sign. As the week wore on, she began to lose hope. They did not wish to know her. She should not have written at all. She would not expect a letter now.

But on the sixth day, the servant placed a letter into her hands, in handwriting that had once been so dear and familiar to her.

The address was unfamiliar, so they had moved! Perhaps that accounted for the delay.

'Dearest, dearest Caroline, (That was a good start, Caroline thought, her heart beginning to feel the first drops of relief.)

As you can see from the address above, we have moved to Kensington. How wonderful it was to hear that you are alive and well. Your brother Percy and I were elated beyond telling. I had to send a servant to his office on Tuesday to tell him to come home directly. Before I proceed, your dear Uncle passed to Eternal Life three years ago, so we moved to make way for the new rector. By then, Percy, who by great fortune and no little hard work, was in a position to make a home for me and my children. He and his dear wife ("Percy is married!" was Caroline's sudden exclamation, causing the other women to look up in surprise.) *her name is Bella, are all kindness to us. The children are at boarding school. I have shared your letter with Percy and Bella. I am sure you do not mind, but as your brother, he is closer to you in law than I.*

WE BEG YOU TO COME HOME. In any case, we intend to call upon you next Sunday at three o'clock, as you will surely have received this letter by then. You will be ready to come home with us next Sunday? Please say YES. Do not be afraid or ashamed in any way. The information you gave us will not go outside us three, soon to be four after Sunday, I hope, at 14 Holland Way. We will think up a tale for everybody to explain your absence over the last several years. In any case, few people know us here in Kensington, and I have never divulged that Percy had a sister. It was too painful and too complicated a situation to talk of, and inevitably led to speculation and discussions distressing to me and to your brother. There is so much more. My pen runs away with me. We lost dear little Archibald, to whooping cough.'

They have had sorrows too, thought Caroline.

Caroline walked about in a dream all day. *Was it possible,* she thought, *that she could go home again?*

Her aunt had mentioned that Percy had done very well, but forgotten to tell her how, and there was so much more she wished to know. How had her beloved Uncle died? She was infused with a great longing for Sunday, but she lay awake on Saturday night, full of fears in that strange zone between waking and sleeping, when reason fades and terrors are heightened.

She would have changed, and they would not know her. Her clothes were shabby, worse than any of their servants wore on Sundays. Only her hat was passable. She had lost her refined ways, and she could not remember anything of what Miss Beale had taught her of manners and deportment. She would not fit in. Everyone would whisper, and the servants would snigger and talk about her downstairs.

Eventually she fell asleep. On Sunday, she went to church and felt calmer. After dinner, she got dressed in her best and waited in the drawing room with Mrs. May, as she had begged her to be present when they arrived. Why had she not asked Mrs. May to take her to Kensington, instead of meeting them here? She was suddenly ashamed of everything and everybody around her, and then felt ashamed for being ashamed.

The clock struck three, a carriage drew up outside. Peering through the net curtains, Caroline saw an older woman alight, look briefly about her, and come to the front door. Aunt Mary! She ached to answer the doorbell herself. but no, everything had to be done properly. Moments later her aunt was shown in. Every protocol forgotten, Caro ran to her and threw herself into her arms, sobbing uncontrollably.

rthur read the note again as he walked toward Pearl Lane. He had received it on Friday, and it plunged him into a maelstrom of feeling. Grief, because he was losing Caroline for good. A happy feeling also, for he loved her and wanted the best for her.

Dear Arthur, I have been in contact with my family in Kensington where they now live, and they are willing to take me home! You can only guess at the joy this brings me. They will call for me on Sunday at 3pm. I know that's the time you come to call on Eleanor, and I do hope you can meet them.

Rejoice with me, Arthur, as this is what I have longed for but it was so far out of my reach, I had given up all hope. I will never forget your kindness to me.

Sincerely, Caroline Davey

'It's like when someone suffers a great deal before death,' he thought to himself as he folded the note again and turned in to Pearl Lane. 'You don't want to lose them, but you want their suffering to be over, no matter what the loss to oneself.'

There was a carriage in the lane, practically filling it. The children were loudly admiring it, and the boy who had the charge of the reins was preening in the responsibility, charging a farthing to anybody who wanted to hold the reins with him for a minute.

Aunt Mary was surprised to find a grown woman hurtling herself into her arms. It was, of course, her niece, now so much older, with no trace of girlhood left.

"I thought I'd never see you again," sobbed Caroline, and Aunt Mary felt a little uncomfortable. Such displays of emotion were not common among adult people, but she rapidly made allowances for her niece, who had been through an ordeal, the hardships of which she could only guess at. She returned the embrace warmly. Every allowance should be made for Caroline.

But she looked so poor! Her gown and shawl were of the cheapest materials, though they had a distinct flair and fashion. Her box, a common box used by servants, was on a chair. It occurred to Mary then that she and Percy had planned this homecoming without a thought. The story they had told the servants, that Miss Davey was returning from a long stay in Devonshire, would not hold up.

"Where's Percy?" Caroline asked through her tears.

Percy bounded into the room, looked around briefly for his sister, and brought himself up short when he realised that it was the woman with tear-stained eyes who was staring at him.

"Forgive me. It's been years."

"I would hardly have known you either," replied Caroline, embracing him only a little less fiercely than she had her aunt. The tears came again.

"And Mrs. Davey?"

"She stayed at home. It was better that just Auntie Mary and I come. You will like her, Caroline. She is as good and tenderhearted a woman as ever walked the earth."

Caroline then remembered her manners and introduced Mrs. May. Aunt Mary thanked her profusely for the care of Caroline. Though she knew little about it, it was clear that but for her intervention, her niece would still be lost to her.

Mrs. May invited the visitors to sit and pressed them to take tea. There was a little hesitation, but upon Caroline's echoing the request, they all sat and Aunt May rang the bell.

Miss Ellis entered then, and Caroline introduced her to Mrs. Barton and Mr. Davey as 'my particular friend.' Eleanor seemed anxious that the visitors not view her as any common woman and spoke in an accent which bespoke her upbringing and education, which Caroline thought a little pitiful, and displayed the etiquette of a gentlewoman, sitting bolt upright in her chair.

Arthur arrived moments later. He was received with every cordiality, and if he was a little quiet, nobody really noticed.

REMAKING CAROLINE

The tea was taken, and it was time to take leave. Arthur shook Caroline's hand with a warmth that flooded her heart with fondness and gratitude. Eleanor's farewell was said in tears of thanks for her rescue. Before they left, most of the other girls and women flocked to the narrow hall to say goodbye, and then she was whisked away in the carriage with her aunt, as Percy drove.

"Aunt Mary, I'm very shabby," owned Caroline, pinching her skirt. "I am hardly fit to be seen in your home. What will the servants think?"

Mary was very relieved that Caroline had brought it up.

"We don't want them to look down on you, Caroline, and gossip, and make inquiries, so we will have to do something. I have an idea. You and I will stay at a hotel for a few days, and I will have you outfitted. This is the only solution. Your past must not be known to anybody, and there must be no room for speculation. Are you agreeable?"

Caroline nodded. Aunt Mary called to Percy and he dismounted as she laid out her plan. As it happened, it was an excellent time for Caroline and her aunt to become reacquainted before she went to Kensington. They were on neutral ground and Caroline disclosed to her aunt details that she would not tell her brother and sister-in-law. Mary was distressed beyond imagining but tried not to show it.

A good dressmaker known to the Hotel was employed to make her three gowns. They went shopping on Bond Street, where Mary bought her an Indian muslin and a Paisley shawl. New boots and a pair of good shoes were found, and corsets, petticoats, and nightgowns followed. Every vestige of her old life was abandoned. She must keep her hat though. She had made it herself and would not be parted from it.

She was a gentlewoman arrived from Devon, although an illness had delayed her by a few days, and Aunt Mary had 'gone to Devon and fetched her.' Whether the servants really believed this or not did not matter. What was important was that she showed no trace of her years with low and criminal people in the worst areas of London.

Snuggling into the scented sheets that night in a chamber with velvet bedcurtains, Caroline drifted happily to sleep. She was home. Surely everything would be excellent from now on. She would not marry. She'd live with her brother and sister-in-law and their children forever. She had been re-created. Her secret would never be known.

FIRST DIFFICULTIES

The change in circumstances held difficulties unforeseen by Caroline or by her family.

Her first feeling was an unexpected anger at the years that had been stolen from her. She should be married now and have her own establishment and a family. But even though she had lost so much, she was very proud of and happy for Percy. He had lost all his former interest in the law, and instead he had trained as an accountant in a thriving firm and had married the owner's daughter, Bella, who had fallen in love with him as soon as she had seen him, and persuaded her father to favour him. Bella was his only child, and he had given them a fine house as a wedding present.

Percy poured out his guilt at his own perceived neglect of her in Surrey Gardens. He had blamed himself for years and still regretted that he had become distracted by his garrulous schoolfellow. They had searched frantically for her that evening, and called the police, who after an unsuccessful search had suggested a missing person's notice in the newspapers. That they had done, with no good lead except a number of people had come forward to say there had been a suspicious-looking man in the Park, staring at the young ladies, and who had moved along as soon as he was noticed. They had concluded that he had abducted Caroline. As weeks turned into months and years, her death seemed more probable.

"To think you were not five miles off," wept Aunt Mary one evening when they were all gathered together. It seemed worse that she was within reach but undiscovered, than if she had been shipped away to Constantinople. Caroline remembered the voices calling to her in the night, becoming fainter and fainter as she had desperately tried to find her way out. She had not thought of that for a long time, and the renewal of the subject upset her, but she bore it, realising that for her family it was also a tremendously difficult time. Bella seemed uneasy.

She was very sweet but a little awkward in her manner toward her for a few weeks. Caroline tried to understand. Bella had never met a woman like her before. But she was very solicitous of her needs, as was her aunt.

Her late uncle had claimed her one hundred pounds extracted from the Sheltons on her eighteenth birthday, and Percy had seen that it was invested wisely. It was no great fortune and would not attract any wealthy suitor, but she felt she was wealthy. Percy was very generous to her, making her a dress allowance of thirty pounds a year. To Caroline, it was a vast sum of money.

And yet, when she should have felt very happy, she found herself sinking into an indescribable sadness she could not explain.

She missed her friends, the Ellises and Glennons in particular. She could not speak of any of them to her family. They turned the subject when she began. Whitechapel was left behind. A gracious Georgian house was now her home, with its scrubbed doorsteps and polished railings, five servants, and every luxury inside. She wrote to her friends and posted the letters herself, as the footman would find it odd that she was writing to anybody in

Whitechapel. She saw that Aunt Mary and Bella did not share her delight at receiving replies, though Percy tried.

"The new girl, rescued from a horrible man, is learning to grow vegetables. There is a little garden, you know, in the back, but you did not see it."

"And Daphne has settled in. She was so frail and frightened when she arrived! I'm glad she has found friends."

"Oh no! I have very bad news! Miss Ellis, Eleanor, left without saying a word to anybody. What can be the matter with her? That's why she did not reply to my letter. Where can she have gone to? I wonder what Arthur thinks. He must be anxious. I hope she hasn't taken to drink again."

"Is it not time to leave all their worries and anxieties to themselves?" ventured Aunt Mary kindly. "You are not among them anymore."

"No, no. I cannot." Caroline's face grew a little red with emotion. How could they not understand that these women were her supports, her friends, and that without them, she might have fallen into utter despair?

"I am sorry, dear." Aunt Mary said hurriedly, picking up the teapot. "Your cup is empty. Have some more tea. It's Twinings. Is it not good?"

But there were many good aspects to being home again. She was with her loved ones, and everything was worth that. The older Barton children, though they did not remember her, were wild for the holidays to come so that they could meet their new cousin. Letters flew to her from them, and she wrote back telling them the memories she had of them, which made her think of Horace Watts. Where was he now, she wondered?

She also enjoyed the easier style of living. What a change it was to have your clothes washed, dried, and ironed for you, to have them laid out for you to wear, to go downstairs to a large breakfast of kippers and sausages and ham and eggs, to eat a sumptuous luncheon, to have afternoon tea, followed by a table groaning with platters of food for dinner? She ate her fill every day and began to put on weight.

One day, soon after she arrived, as she was about to enter the drawing room, she overheard a conversation between her aunt and Bella. They had neglected to shut the door fully.

"But how shall we tell her that her ways are a little uncouth? I do not like to tell her."

"I think we must, Aunt. She eats big mouthfuls as if she were starving, and she slouches in her chair. And my mother presses me to tell her more about her. I will not, but she wonders why Caroline put up such a spirited argument against prison when the subject came up last week. I know she mixed with a very criminal class, and perhaps these friends who write to her are related to somebody."

"It's the man we met, Mr. Ellis, Arthur. Caroline told me that he was imprisoned for seven years for a crime he did not commit. I expect he told her that he was innocent. We must proceed carefully. I wouldn't hurt her for the world."

"Nor I, Aunt!" This was hastily said and sincerely meant, she knew. Caroline felt she should draw away, but could not.

"That sister of his, Miss Ellis. She appeared to have breeding. Now, she's gone again, a very strange woman, that."

"The sooner she forgets them all, Aunt, the better. She has moods of melancholy. I suppose she needs time. Poor Caroline!"

She drew away again and went to play with the dog in the back garden. The dog did not care if she was overeating, slouching, had friends in criminal classes, or anything else.

DINNER PARTY

The invitation to Lady Russell's dinner party included Miss Davey. Caroline felt a little nervous about going. From the few times she had been in company, she had felt on the edge of the party, not really belonging, but on another track with her thoughts and her impressions. In general, she could not enjoy small-talk. Did any of these fine ladies or smooth gentlemen know what trouble was? Had they ever experienced hunger, or cold, or destitution, or had to work hard from dawn to far into the night? Had they ever had to dirty their hands?

Nevertheless, she dressed in her best gown, a mauve silk with ruffled sleeves and white lace flounces. Her hair had soft glossy curls and she wore a gardenia in it. It was pouring heavy rain and had done so for several days, but the ladies stepped lightly around the puddles as they made their way from the carriage to the hall door.

There were about fifty guests, all wonderfully attired. Lady Russell introduced them to several groups of people, and she curtsied very nicely.

It was time for dinner, and Caroline was taken into the dining room by a tall gentleman named Mr. Harries. He was seated beside her and was a pleasant companion, if foppish with his large bow tie and ostentatious cufflinks.

"I find it incredible that you are still a Miss," he said to her with a smooth charm to cover his impertinence. "Why have you not been snatched up in wedlock?"

"Every woman does not have to marry," she said rather rudely.

"Most do, though. Except of course, if they are of large means. Then they may choose their path."

She made no reply, just slashed the roast beef on her plate and speared several pieces onto her fork along with a helping of brussels sprouts. He watched her as she ate heartily. Aunt Mary, across the table, felt her heart sink. Her niece had a vulgar enjoyment of her food, and it gave her away. What would people think?

After dinner, the ladies withdrew while the gentlemen smoked cigars and drank port. Mr. Harries felt compelled to enquire further about Miss Davey from a man he knew to be acquainted with the family. He was far out of Percy's hearing.

"There is some mystery about her," said Mr. Bellington. "They are giving out the story that she spent years in Devonshire, but few believe it. There is a rumour that she wasimprisoned for some crime, for she is known to be dead against it as punishment, and had gotten very emotional when the subject is brought up."

"Very intriguing! I like a woman of mystery, I shall endeavour to find out more."

"You are rather a mystery yourself, are you not, Mr. Harries?" Mr. Drake leaned over in their direction. "You have a new bird of paradise, I hear. Is she as beautiful as the last?"

"That is enough about me, gentlemen."

"On a practical matter, if you wish to ride home in my carriage," said Mr. Drake, "we shall have to leave early. Louise hates to be out after ten."

"Too early for me, Drake. I shall take a cab."

ARTHUR'S PASSENGER

"Cab!"

Arthur halted outside the gracious home in Kensington. The rain poured down, but he was wearing his wide cape which had a hood.

"Where to, Guv'nor?"

"Aylesbury Road, please. And don't dawdle, or go the long way."

In the dark, Arthur only saw a tall man in a greatcoat, but he recognised the voice immediately. It was the voice that had sealed his fate when he was sixteen years old. He was sure of it. It was Gregory Harries. He could never forget that voice!

The carriage door slammed shut. He was inside.

"Walk on," he called to the horses, and they set off at a brisk trot. Arthur's feelings were hard to describe. They were a mixture of anger, deep resentment, bitterness, and betrayal. He suffered anew the same anguish he had suffered during the first years after his sentencing. The reason for his suffering was in the cab, sitting back, out of the rain, probably with a stomach full of good food and wine, and now nodding off. He had done all right for himself! Arthur had had a vestige of comfort thinking that Gregory Harries was either dead or destitute, but neither was the case. Harries had also ruined his sister and caused his family to flee, and those were only a few of the sins against him.

He did not go toward Aylesbury. He went instead along to an area he knew, to a lane that ended in a disgusting pile of refuse. It was at the end of a hill, and every bit of debris and litter from the slope and its gutters made its way there in heavy rain, causing a lake of rubbish and filth to clog the drain.

When he reached there, he stopped, jumped off the box, and wrenched open the door.

"I say, are we there?" began Mr. Harries.

Arthur reached in and grabbed him by the lapels of his greatcoat, pulled him from the carriage, and threw him into the lake of mud and dirt. The stench was overpowering.

"Help! Murder! Murder!" shouted Gregory as he sloshed about, covered in mud and dirt, trying to get a foothold on the slimy ground. "I say, don't kill me! If it's money you want, here!" He reached a muddy hand into his inner pocket.

"You're fortunate I haven't killed you, you scoundrel!" Arthur said angrily. "Wallow in that muck for a while, for you belong there!"

"What, who?" Gregory began to pick himself up. "Who are you? What do you want?

Arthur heard the policeman's rattle so he took the reins and guided the horses down a side street he knew that would lead him back to the main road undetected. He knew every nook and cranny of the area.

He should not have done it, he knew, but it had given him great satisfaction, and no harm would result from Gregory Harries having to take a mud bath.

"Where were you? It's four o'clock! What on earth happened to you?" asked Eleanor, when she saw Gregory come in, wet through and smelling like a rat.

"I don't know! Some criminal cab driver took me to somewhere foul, and threw me out of the cab and into a filthy mess. I suppose the intent was robbery, but the police were coming so he made off."

"What was he like?" asked Eleanor, taking off his coat. "Ugh, what a disgusting smell! How did you get home?"

"The policeman told me I was in some rotten hole named Gullseye by the docklands. But there were no cabs down there. So I had to walk! When I finally met a cab, nobody would take me, as they said I was too soiled! Get Jenny up! I need a bath!"

Eleanor went out to awaken the servant to heat water.

"What did he look like, this cabbie?"

"I don't know. I only got a glimpse of him! He had his hood pulled down of course. He just reached in, grabbed me, and threw me out! London is not a safe place, is it?"

"Was it somebody you knew, perhaps?"

"How could it be? He seemed to know me, but how could I know any cab driver?" he asked crossly, as she took his shirt and dropped it on the ground. "That shirt cost me fifteen shillings! It's ruined! The world is full of criminals, and nobody is safe anywhere anymore. I have a good mind to go to abroad again!"

"Did he say anything? That he wanted to rob you, for instance?"

"No! He just said I was fortunate he had not killed me! I wish I had taken note of the company the cab belongs to, but I did not. The police were no help."

"Perhaps he thought you were someone else," she soothed him.

Eleanor gave the clothes to Jenny, who was cross at having to get up so early, get a fire going, and heat enough water for the hip-bath. She also did not like taking orders from a *mistress*, but kept her lips shut tight about that.

Eleanor smiled a delighted smile to herself when she was alone. *'Good for you, Arthur,'* she giggled.

81

LOVE REKINDLED

G regory Harries could not get Miss Davey out of his head. He had never met a girl like her, and, of course, she was wealthy. There was no other reason a girl chose not to marry, in his opinion.

It had taken three days and as many hot scented baths to get the smell from his person. He sulked for those days, and had to stay in. Eleanor fussed over him like a mother hen. She really was a fool, but very useful.

The following week, he donned a morning suit to pay a call to the Davey home in Kensington. He would court Miss Davey. Eleanor was not for marrying, of course. They had met accidentally on the street one day, and he being without female company, had apologised for his past sins and invited her to stay with him. He was using her, of course, but she was resigned to that. She expected no more from him now than to be his mistress.

He had asked her for news of Arthur, and Eleanor said that she did not have any, not for years. He supposed he was doing very well for himself now, much better than if he had succeeded his father as rector of Middledene, and he had done a good thing for him, in that case. Eleanor agreed. What a stupid woman she was.

He had not spoken to Matthew for years, nor his parents, but he still expected to be heir. He had made a lot of money in Monte Carlo and other places on the continent. He was a skilled card shark, but did not want to sully his name in England, so had to look around for a better means of support. As it was, there were a few clubs in London he could not venture into again.

He would marry soon, for money, and if the fortune came in an attractive package, he would have no objection. Miss Davey intrigued him.

As he strode along the busy street he heard his name. He turned around to see a friend hailing him, a man he played cards with sometimes, who had not yet found out that he was a cheat. He was a barrister at law and had been in Scotland on holidays recently.

"Ah, Watts. Have you returned from Edinburgh, then?"

"It's not my ghost, Harries. Are we going the same way? Where are you off to?"

"I'm paying a call upon a lady who I think I shall marry someday."

"Think? Who is she?"

"I'm not very sure. She says she is a Miss Davey, Caroline Davey. She lives with her brother in Kensington."

"Miss Davey!" Horace caught himself before he could say too much. "I know the family," he said casually, though his head was spinning. "If you don't think me a third wheel, I would like to come along."

"You are welcome. I would like your opinion."

Watts could not believe his luck. Miss Davey, Caroline, his first love, was back! He had thought that her aunt had found out about them and that she had been spirited away. But she was back now, and still *Miss Davey*. Henry, however, was confident of winning her hand. He felt confident that as soon as

Caroline saw him, her old love for him would return. Harries had an inflated view of himself and of his charms. It would give him satisfaction to snatch his choice from under his friend's nose.

It was with these thoughts that he was, together with Mr. Harries, shown into the drawing room at Holland Way.

"Mr. Harries and Mr. Watts," they were announced, and Caroline, who was trimming a hat, looked up quickly at the name she knew. A deep flush came over her as she observed Mr. Horace Watts. She stood up and began to tremble a little. Was it really Horace Watts?

How often, in those early days of her captivity, had she thought of him, longed for him? She had even imagined a scenario where he found out where she was and effected a rescue and carried her to safety, dodging bullets and spears and angry dogs. But her dreams had dissolved there, because he would walk away when he inevitably found out what she was. No man was that generous and good.

But here was Horace now. Yes, the same Horace. He was staring at her and she at him, and everybody seemed to be staring at them.

Gregory knew immediately his quest was in vain. That was sneaky of Watts! Aunt Mary wondered how they knew each other. Bella saw a future for poor Caroline. This man seemed to be in a trance as he advanced, took her hand, and kissed it.

Caroline sat down, hardly the mistress of her emotions, and Mr. Watts seated himself beside her.

82
FUTURE PLANS

For the next weeks, Caroline was happier than she had ever been, but for one tormenting thought. If Horace asked for her hand in marriage, she would have to inform him of what had truly happened to her. He would most likely draw away.

They drove out together, they walked together, and they talked a great deal. Horace always decided where they would go, and he always decided what she would like to eat and drink. But she was still in love with him and felt that she was a girl again, and that loving him could perhaps wipe away the intervening years between fifteen and twenty-three. Those years had never happened.

Sometimes she thought of Arthur, but he was in her past now. She could never marry Arthur. But she did not think she would ever have a friend like him again, male or female. Their common experiences had bonded them together.

"I thought that today, you might like to listen to me at Court," said Horace one day. "I'm prosecuting a murder case. Would you like to hear it?" Before she could answer, he said, "Of course you would. Bring your Aunt or Mrs. Davey with you. I promise you it will be very interesting."

They went and sat in the Gallery. Caroline was not persuaded that the defendant was guilty. Horace's cross-examination of him was brutal. She supposed it had to be done that way. He was found guilty and sentenced to hang.

"Was not that wonderful?" said Harold outside, his black gown flapping about him in the breeze.

"How were you so sure that he was guilty?" she asked him.

"Were you not listening, Caroline? I proved the case."

"But how were you sure?"

"Be quiet! Look, look. Judge Dudley-Grace. My Lord," he bowed deeply to a gentleman passing by who took absolutely no notice of him. "Now, ladies, if you will do me the honour of lunching with me, there is a quiet hotel just around the corner."

Later, Caroline was thoughtful. Horace certainly set her heart beating, but his way of interrupting and lording it over her annoyed her. Would she be able to get used to it?

83

THE TRUTH

Caroline dressed in her cobalt silk with white satin stripes, a particular favourite of Horace's. Its skirt was full but not a full crinoline, for he detested full crinolines and said they made women look ridiculous. They were going for a walk in Kensington Park, and he had intimated that he had an important question to ask her.

If he did, she then had to tell him the truth.

He escorted her to the Park, and they walked there, along the tree-lined paths, until they came to a wrought-iron park bench set in a leafy bower, where he indicated they should sit. He took out his handkerchief and dusted the bench before seating her. He sat beside her and took her hands in his.

"You know the question I am about to ask, Caro. Will you do me the great honour of becoming my wife?"

She had not even opened her mouth to respond before he went on, "I was thinking of September next. Would you have time to get your trousseau ready? As for your wedding gown, there is a fad to wear white. I do not like it as much as blue. A blue gown, such as you have on today, but paler, perhaps, as that is a little too blue. Brides should wear pale colours."

"Wait, wait!" Caroline cried out. "Wait, I have not made you my answer yet!"

He looked amazed. "Caroline, you have given me every encouragement, please do not say now that, what? You must tell me something? What could you possibly have to tell me?"

"Please just listen, I beg you, Horace, just be quiet for a while. I cannot enter into marriage with anybody without being honest. This is very difficult for me." She began to weep.

"Oh come now, Caro, it can't be that bad. As to fortune, I'm indifferent."

"It is worse than bad." She found the words and told him. He looked utterly shocked, distressed, and for the first time in his life, without speech. He got up and walked away, turning his back upon her.

Now I have done it, she thought. *He wants no more to do with me.*

"Are you speaking the truth?" he whirled around.

"Ask my brother, my aunt, even the police if you like."

"But that's egregious, I remember the case, where the women were tried. They were horrid witches. And you were one of their unsuspecting victims! Oh Caroline!" He dropped down beside her once again, took her hand, and kissed it.

"I'm sure this information will cause you to alter your plans," she said quietly.

"No," he said firmly. "Not one whit. I still want to marry you, though you are, or have been though…" He seemed lost for words. "How many, Caroline? How many men?"

"Do not ask me that!" She got up, took her parasol, and walked hurriedly away, in tears. She turned around again. "You must never mention it. Never.

Our children, if we are blessed, must never know. Your family must never know. Nobody but you."

"Of course, of course. I am truly sorry, I am." He said, catching up with her. "But I still have not had your answer."

"It is yes." She smiled through her tears and he kissed her.

84

HORACE

Horace could not get the matter out of his mind. As he strode home, his feelings for Caroline began to alter. Like all of London, he had felt a great deal of compassion for the girls trapped by the Wicked Women of Gullseye when the matter had been in the newspapers. Everybody had condemned them and exonerated the young women. When Caroline had owned to him that she was one of them, he had been overcome also, by astonishment followed by the appropriate reaction, that of a well-bred gentleman, reacting with a generosity of heart, saying it would not matter at all.

He put his key in the door and let himself in, and going upstairs to change for dinner, he acknowledged that this revelation put his engagement in a very different complexion.

He did not now want to marry Caroline Davey. She was now in every way objectionable. But he was entangled. He could not break off the engagement, for a gentleman did not. He was trapped now.

Over the next twenty-four hours, his attitude turned over slowly from compassion to contempt.

She will never end the engagement, he thought wretchedly. *She considers herself very fortunate indeed to have me. And I'm stuck with her. I shall have to make the best of it, I suppose. She doesn't even have a fortune to sweeten the deal. However, she shall always do my bidding in our life together. She owes me that. I shall be very strict with her, she will not be able to go anywhere without my express permission, and she must always be accompanied by a servant who will report on everywhere she goes and everybody she meets. Otherwise, if we have a child, how will I be sure it's mine? She must spend her life being grateful to me for rescuing her from her wretched state, for if I had not proposed marriage, she would surely have gone back to her old life. She will not be allowed any alcohol, for that's the ruin of many wives, and she is probably very partial to it already. As to an allowance, she shall account for every penny she spends, lest it goes on the cheap and tawdry frivolities she has been used to. I shall decide the education of our children, especially the girls. And servants, I shall have to direct that also. There's a danger she might engage some of her old friends, criminals who will prey on her sympathy or even try to blackmail her. I will choose them.*

'She will be happy because I married her knowing what she was. She ought to expect no more than that. If she forgets, I will remind her. I would never like to strike a woman, but what if blows be the only language she understands?'

85

BEEZLE CLUB

"Are you not going out tonight, Gregory?"

"No, I'm not." Gregory sprawled on the bed. He was in his shirt sleeves and held a bottle of spirits to his lips. A red-lined cloak was thrown over a chair.

"Not going to the Beezle, then?"

"No. I'm never going there again."

"Ah, they caught you."

"Yes. I was thinking, Ellie, about taking a ship to America. I think I'd do well in America, in the West. Will you come?"

She knew he meant none of it, but she said, "If you need me, Gregory dear, I will come."

"You're so loyal. I don't deserve you."

She sat in the rocking chair watching him as he emptied the bottle and fell asleep. He would sleep until morning. She got up and put on her shawl and went out. She had no fear of the streets. Years of her hard life there had taught her how to look out for herself. She walked quickly in the direction of Jermyn Street and the Beezle Club, which was not its real name. Above the door spelled the words, TOWER HOTEL. She reached the door about nine o'clock and pulled the bell. It opened, and revealed the butler, who frowned when he saw her.

"If you're looking for Red Cloak, he isn't here."

"I know he isn't. That's why I've come. I need to see G.J."

He hesitated, so she pushed past him and went up the stairs, where there were several tables where men were engaged in cards. There was a heavy smell of beer and opium drifting from the back room. She walked past the men, who hardly noticed her, and found the man she was looking for at a table by himself, poring over an account book by the light of a candle. He shut it smartly when she reached him.

"You! Red Cloak's moll! How dare you show your face here," he said, getting up.

"I come as your friend," she said, smiling. "I know he cheated last night, and I know what you wish to do, what you always do, with cheaters."

He was surprised, and he motioned her to sit opposite him.

"I know you employ a few hefty thugs to follow him and break a few bones, but I want to tell you a story first," began Eleanor.

TRUE COLOURS

Percy wanted his beloved sister to have the most beautiful wedding in the world, and whatever she wished. He gave her and her aunt a great deal of money to accomplish this.

"When I was a little girl, I wanted a big wedding, and a gown with yards and yards of lace and organdie, everything Mamma had," she said to Aunt Mary. "Now, I can have what I dreamed for then!"

"Your brother is most generous," Aunt Mary said warmly. "It's beautiful to see him so considerate of his sister's happiness."

"We only had each other after Mama died."

There was only one grief for Caroline, and that was that she could not invite her friends from

Whitechapel. Also, how would Arthur take the news that she was getting married? He would be disappointed, heartbroken perhaps. But he would have to forget her. *And where was Eleanor?*

The engaged couple were now allowed to spend time alone. One day, Horace called upon her when everybody was out. They sat in the drawing room, and he spoke of the house he was buying, a two-story in Chelsea, which was becoming a fashionable place to live.

"I should like to see it," said Caroline with excitement.

"No, allow it to be a surprise. I know what you like." Horace sprawled on the couch, his head in her lap. "I say, Caro, with everybody out, I think we could have a little hanky-panky, couldn't we?"

"Hanky-panky?" Caroline said, pretending not to understand.

He sprang up and grabbed her, pushing her back on the couch, pinning her underneath him.

"Horace, stop. We aren't married yet. Stop."

"What does that matter, Caroline? To you, I mean? We don't have to wait for the wedding!"

"Why not? Why not? And whatever do you mean, *to me*? If I were Miss Anybody Else, you would wait for the wedding!"

"Well I don't see why we should wait," he began to kiss her. She felt a resurgence of the terrified feelings that she had on her first nights at Mrs. Tait's, the feelings that she was caught, trapped, helpless. She struggled to get free.

He began to utter words that no lady should hear. He spoke in a way that many of the men she had been forced to lie with spoke, ugly, disgusting names for her. She reached back and her hand found the bell. She pulled it down as hard as she could.

"I have summoned a servant!" she managed to shout, as she struggled.

He rolled away, and got up. He was flushed and very angry.

"Why? What's wrong with you?"

"There's nothing wrong with me." As Caroline said it, she knew it to be true, as true as the earth was round. *There was nothing wrong with her.* "But I realise that you will never see me as a woman with dignity. To you, I will always be a prostitute. But I'm not. I never have been, in my heart and in my soul! God knows that, God knows my innocence! God knows I am still a virgin in my heart! Take your ring." She wrenched it off her finger and threw it at him.

The door opened.

"Yes, Miss Davey?"

"Mr. Watts is just leaving now," she said stiffly, trying to smooth down her hair. "Show him out." He took up the ring which had landed on the floor and left.

CONFESSION!

"Liverpool. We could travel, but I need money for that. I haven't got any money, and I cannot go out, because G.J. will set thugs upon me." Gregory was drinking another bottle of brandy and smoking opium. "Why are you at the window, Ellie? Why do you keep looking out?"

"I want to see if Mrs. Benn has sent for the midwife. She told me today that she thought her time was coming."

"Oh, all right. That sort of affair is a complete unknown to me."

He fell asleep. She continued her vigil until she saw the signal, a lamp waved three times at the corner. She sped downstairs and opened the door.

G.J. entered, accompanied by a well-dressed man, with his hat pulled down. Two other men lurked in the shadows, and she saw the gleam of steel in the bars they carried.

"I doubt there will be a need for those," she said. She did not want a violent outcome.

"Stay here. We'll whistle if we need you," said G.J.

She led the two men upstairs and threw open the door.

"Gregory! Wake up! You have visitors!"

He rose slowly, blinking and scowling. A look of dread came upon him and he lunged for the window, only to be caught by G.J., who flung him onto a chair.

"Why did you let them in, Ellie?" he asked plaintively.

She took a document from her pocket and unfolded it.

"I had this drawn up a few days ago. You have to sign it. If you do not, these two men might make you."

"Ellie," he wailed, like a child. "What are you doing? I thought you loved me."

"You think I love you? I grew out of it. You helped me in that. You've ruined my brother's life. And my family's, and mine. It was Arthur, by the way, who threw you out of the cab that night into the mud. How I laughed when I was alone!"

"So he did come back. You lied to me," he whimpered. "I never loved you. If I told you I did, I was lying too."

"I have not loved you for years, Gregory, so your words do not affect me in the least."

"Could you keep this argument for another time, perhaps?" asked G.J., irritated. "I'm in a hurry. Are you going to sign the lady's document or not?"

"What the devil is it?" He snatched it up and read it by the light of a candle, tore it into pieces, upon which Eleanor reached into her pocket for another.

"Don't tear this one up," snarled G.J. "Sit down and sign it."

Eleanor uncapped the inkwell and dipped the pen into it, shook the excess ink off the nib, and held it out to him.

"This is most unfair," whined Gregory.

"Sign it," said the Boss, taking out his pocket-watch. "I will give you five seconds to begin. Five."

"What interest do you have in my signing it?"

"*Four.* This lady told me a story that would make an executioner weep. *Three.* I agreed that instead of the usual punishment meted out to cheats, that I'd make you sign this document confessing to your evil deed. If you don't, we will do the usual. *Two.*"

"But this could put me in prison," complained Gregory.

"I want Arthur's name to be cleared. That's all I want. After you have signed it, leave London, leave England. It is all the same to me."

"*One!*" roared the Boss.

"All right, all right, you are all against me." He took the pen, and signed it. Eleanor heard the scratching sound as if it were the most beautiful music in the world.

Eleanor signed as a witness, and the man that the Boss had brought with him, a lawyer who owed him a favour, notarised it.

Eleanor applied the powder to dry it and held it in her hands.

"We'll be off," said G.J. "You got off lightly, thanks to the lady here. You never come to my club again."

"I am ready to leave also," Eleanor said. She took her cloak and hat and taking her packed box from the hallway, hurried away into the night, and went straight to Arthur's lodging. He was there and was very surprised to see her.

"Eleanor, you at last! Where have you been? I was at my wits' end. Why are you smiling like that?"

"I have good news! Turn up your lamp high. Look here, read it!"

He sat down and read it and was quiet and still, as if he hardly dared to believe the words. Then he read it again, aloud.

I, Gregory James Harries, of Middledene House, Middledene, Nottinghamshire, wish to state the following:

That on the night of July 18th, 1846, I stole a box of silver and gold coins from Mr. Humphrey Leamy, Blacksmith, of Middledene Village.

That I planted a navy-blue cap belonging to Arthur Ellis, son of the Rector of Middledene Church of England Parish, in Mr. Leamy's house.

Furthermore, that I lied in court, under oath, about overhearing Arthur Ellis state that he was going to rob Mr. Leamy. I never heard him utter such a statement.

That Mr. Arthur Ellis is innocentt of the robbery and assault of Mr. Leamy, and that I am guilty of the robbery and assault of Mr. Leamy.

Given under my hand this day of eighteen hundred and sixty, in the presence of two witnesses.

Signed: Gregory James Harries

Witness One: Miss Eleanor Maria Ellis

Witness Two: Mr. Cyril Joseph Blake, Lawyer, Notary.

"How did you accomplish this?"

"Do not ask, Arthur. I accomplished it. That is all you need to know."

"I must return to the lodging before it closes for the night," Eleanor said. To herself she added, *'I will write to Caroline immediately!'*

JOY

The post was usually delivered at breakfast, and two days later Caroline had a pleasant surprise, a letter in familiar handwriting.

"It's from Eleanor Ellis, I know! So she is safe!"

Aunt Mary and Bella looked up, as did her brother Percy.

"That's good news," he said. "Good news indeed."

She tore it open. Her eyes scanned it with increasing joy and she jumped up from the table, almost taking the tablecloth with her in her haste.

"Gregory Harries was found and confessed to the crime! Arthur will get his pardon! He will be fully exonerated! Oh, this is the happiest day!"

They murmured that it was wonderful news indeed.

"Oh, I want to dance for joy!" She whirled about, clutching the letter to her breast. Bella and Aunt Mary exchanged a glance.

"I must write back to her straightaway," Caroline said.

"But you have not finished your breakfast!" said Bella.

In response, Caro picked up her cup of coffee, drank it all back with a noisy slurp, and set it down upon the saucer with a rattle.

"I'm finished now," she said.

"Are you coming to the Fitzgeralds with us?" asked Aunt Mary.

"Oh! No, if you don't mind. I would rather stay and write to Eleanor. I'm so glad she is safe and sound, and that she didn't take to the streets again! I was afraid of that, and that she'd gone back on the drink." Caroline left the room.

There was a pause before Aunt Mary spoke.

"The children will be home for the holidays soon." In that sentence, everybody knew her meaning. The servant came in then with a hot dish for the sideboard.

"Why did she end the engagement?" Bella asked, not noticing her. "She would not divulge, except that she knew that she could never be happy with him. Something happened."

The servant kept silence. Everybody downstairs knew that Mr. Watts had tried to take liberties not his to take before they were married. Sarah had heard the shouting before she opened the drawing room door and saw how rumpled her hair was.

BACK TO WHITECHAPEL

So intent was Caroline in a corner of the parlour writing her response to Eleanor in a series of dizzy exclamation marks that she did not hear her aunt and sister-in-law leave the house. Her brother had left before them. She wrote and rewrote and then stood up suddenly, slamming down her pen.

"I don't want to write a letter," she complained to the bureau as she slammed it shut. "I want to see them! I want to see Arthur, and today, while he's still overcome with the novelty of it all! Why should I not go to them? I will go to them!"

She got her cloak and hat, pulled gloves onto her hands, and set off, shutting the front door behind her. It was a bright day. Or did everything suddenly seem brighter?

She boarded an omnibus, and when it had reached the last stop, got out and walked the rest of the way to Whitechapel. Arthur could be anywhere in London with his cab, but she scanned every one she saw. She reached Bethany Lodging for Women and was greeted there with cries of welcome. She shook off her cloak and sat down to the table while Bess scurried to make tea. Eleanor was there, beaming. The two women embraced like sisters.

"Where is Arthur?"

"He will be here very soon! For we are to go to a lawyer, and set his pardon in motion. No, do not ask me how it was done. That shall be my secret."

As they spoke, the front doorbell rang.

"That is he! Come, you shall accompany us!"

Caroline did not need a second invitation. She wrapped her cloak about her again and bounded after Eleanor.

Arthur was dressed in his best suit. She had never seen him look so handsome. He doffed his hat in greeting. His face was lit up, and when he saw Caroline, his happiness overflowed.

"Arthur!" she said, "I could not wait to see you! I can't tell you how happy I am. At last, you will be exonerated in public!"

He took her hands in his. Eleanor discreetly stepped back a little.

"How are you, Caro? Are you happy, where you are?"

"No, not at all, I miss everybody, and most of all, I miss you, Arthur. I miss you." Her dark eyes misted, and she came closer to him. They wrapped their arms around each other.

Eleanor tip-toed into the hall, out of sight, and closed the door quietly.

"**P**oor Mr. Leamy died a few years ago," Arthur laid the letter down. "But for the last years of his life, an anonymous donor set him up in a little cottage with a housekeeper. He spent his last years comfortably."

"Who could that have been?" asked Caroline.

"No idea. I say, Caroline, would you like to come to Nottingham with Eleanor and me? We shall go next week."

"Of course, I would love to come!"

Caroline had left her life in Kensington behind. They had all said a sorrowful goodbye, and Percy was most affected by it. She moved back to Whitechapel, and she stayed in a good lodging in Merborough Street, which her brother paid for. From there, she was to begin her own charity work. She felt well qualified to help girls and women who had, for whatever reason, found themselves with little option but to sell themselves.

They travelled by train and reached Nottingham by nightfall. Eleanor was very quiet, remembering her downfall there. The following day, they set out for Middledene, passing Hempley, where Arthur pointed out the prison. It was now Arthur's turn to feel downhearted. So much had passed since, so many years, so much sorrow!

And so on to Middledene, walking, relieved to see the bell-tower marking that they were very near. Eleanor remarked on the Norris' gate still half-off its hinges, the Fenwick's impeccably thatched cottage, and the new houses added. Past the bend in the road bringing them to the village street, the old Ellis home looked as it always had, but the rhododendron was an even bigger encroachment on the lawn. They passed it in silence, the sister and brother with their own thoughts and painful realisations. A few children played noisily on the street, stopping to stare at the strangers for a few moments. The butcher looked out his door, squinting, the better to see the strangers, and beckoned to somebody to come and look.

They passed the church and walked from it to the mansion. Such a familiar path to Arthur and Eleanor, it was new to Caroline, but she was drinking in every scene familiar to these two beloved people.

They heard the doorbell ring throughout the house. A younger butler opened it. Lapp must have retired. Arthur gave his name, but he did not know the history of the Ellises, and bid them to enter.

The drawing-room was as it always had been. They were glad to take the weight off their feet, and they sat in silence, all preoccupied with their own thoughts.

The door creaked open. Matthew came in.

MATTHEW'S MISERY

He seemed embarrassed at the company, and did not know where to look. Caroline was introduced, and he greeted her with cordiality. The four sat down and an awkward silence ensued.

"How are your parents?" Eleanor asked gently.

"They are dead."

"I am sorry to hear it," Arthur said.

"I got word that my father was very ill, and returned home immediately. He died two days later. My mother could not stand the shock. She was gone within six months."

They murmured condolences again.

"You are just in the area, on a pleasure trip?" Matthew asked politely. He could hardly meet Arthur's eye.

"No, I have a specific purpose," Arthur said. He reached into his pocket and took out a document.

"I would like you to see this. It is a copy of the original, which is lodged in my lawyer's office in London."

Matthew looked at him briefly, as if wondering why he was being tormented, before he cast his eyes to the sheet of paper.

"Gregory confessed!" he exclaimed. "How did this happen? Where is he now?"

"We do not know, but he is probably where the law cannot find him."

"And, should I leave the country also?" Matthew sounded strained.

"It's not necessary, is it?"

Matthew hung his head. Then he got up and paced the room, finally pausing with his hand on the mantlepiece.

"Covering up for Gregory was the worst thing we ever did. My parents said they did not have a moment's peace after that. They were tormented, as I was. It seems that Gregory was the only one of us who blithely went on with his life. My parents disowned him. I have this pile, but it brings me no joy whatsoever." He glanced at Eleanor. "He hurt you also." She looked down. There was a pause.

"Mr. Leamy?" Arthur asked.

"What do you know of him? He died. After you came here the last time, my parents arranged to have him discharged from the hospital and he lived out his days in a neat little cottage here. They tried to make good the harm they did, at least where he was concerned. But I have offered you no refreshment!" he said then, and striding forward, pulled the bell.

They were very hungry, so did not decline the tea and sandwiches that were offered. The ice between them began to melt.

"But how are you, Matthew?" asked Eleanor unexpectedly.

"I get by. The monks sent me away," he said in a matter-of-fact way. "Because I would not exonerate you, Arthur. They took a great liking to you. The most exciting thing that happened to them all that year was finding you almost frozen in Sherwood Forest. "

"I still have nightmares about Father Marx and his rusty saw that he had since the Battle of Waterloo," Arthur joked, and they all laughed. "Look, Matthew. I truly must say this. You only have one life, and you should seize it with both hands and live it."

Now it was Arthur's turn to pace the room, which he did, cup and saucer in hand. "You were sixteen years old, coerced by your family to lie under oath. I understand the intense pressure."

"I, too, have not had a moment's happiness since then!" he blurted out. "Not one moment! I often wished it was I who had been punished! To have to lie about your best friend to save the brother that you knew was guilty…"

"You can be happy now, with my full permission." Arthur said. "I will be pardoned, they will not come after you, but if they do, I shall ask for leniency. You have paid the price for giving into the unreasonable and criminal demands of your own family. Strive to be happy, Matthew."

"Really? Is that what you think? What you all think?"

"Yes," chorused the ladies.

Matthew brushed away tears.

"Let's all take a little turn around the garden," said Eleanor. "It brought me much joy when I was young, and I would like to show it to Caroline, and we can peer over the wall at the orchard in the parsonage."

NEW PROSPECTS

I n London again, Arthur went back to his job driving a hansom cab. But the weather was dreadful and he had a persistent cough. He began to be bleak about his future as he began to miss days of work. He was concerned in particular about his ability to marry and keep a wife and children.

Caroline was busy with her charity work. She oversaw several little shops and cottage industries and learned all the time. Eleanor helped her. Both women worried about Arthur, and one day Caroline poured out her heart to her Fernleigh friend Clare, now Mrs. Murgatroyd. Her husband Edgar was running for Parliament. He was building his office and employing his staff to run it, and through Clare's intervention, interviewed Mr. Arthur Ellis and engaged him on the spot as Manager. The two men became very good friends. Edgar was elected to Parliament, and when his fortunes increased, so did Arthur's. He was now in a position to marry and have a home, and he and Caroline became engaged. She brought him to meet her relations at Kensington, for they had only had that one short, awkward meeting at the Women's Lodging, and they were very pleased with him. Arthur Ellis was not the criminal they had supposed and had the pardon to prove it.

"Time to plan a wedding again," Aunt Mary said happily.

"I shall be happy with a simple wedding," Caro said.

"You will move back here so we can all become ready together," said Bella with enthusiasm.

There is nothing a family of women love more than to plan a wedding, and Percy observed that he was entirely superfluous to their needs, except to supply the money. "Ribbons! Lace! Flowers!" he exclaimed one day. "I have heard nothing else in this house for the last six weeks!"

But the following morning, a piece of interesting news distracted them.

"Some news that will interest you, Caro! Look!" Percy thrust the newspaper toward his sister.

FERNLEIGH MANOR IN FLAMES
DEVONSHIRE HOUSE BURNED TO THE GROUND

"Uncle Edward's house!"

"I remember it!" said Aunt Mary. "An old place. Read it out, Percival."

"In Devonshire, not forty miles from Exeter, just before dawn on the 1st, a bright light in the western sky alerted a shepherd to the suspicion that a great fire might be burning some miles away. Alerting his employer, Farmer Hopkins, a party of men was formed to go in the direction of the light, and as they drew nearer it became apparent that the source of it was none other than the old house known in the area as Fernleigh Manor. Once owned by the late Colonel Davey, it passed to his niece and nephew, named Shelton, some years ago, and is inhabited by their son, Mr. Howard Shelton, his widowed mother, and his family.

"Upon reaching the venue, spectators saw that there was nothing to be done. The entire structure was in flames. This reporter was on the scene to see the high roof, with its several turrets, crash in an explosion of sparks that drew horrified gasps from the bystanders.

"A friend of the family told this writer that due to the age of the building and its poor state of repair, it had not been possible to insure it, leaving the family at a great financial loss.

"Happily, the family and servants were accounted for and are safe"

"I'm happy nobody was killed or hurt," said Caroline, reflectively. "But I would be lying if I did not say it serves them right. I don't know what they will do now, do you, Percy?"

"They will have to get used to a more modest style of living," he said. "If it had passed to me, I would have repaired it so it would have been eligible for insurance, but there is no point in talking of it. I am happy as I am."

There was no more to be said, and they never mentioned it again. But a few weeks later, a letter arrived in a circuitous way from Miss Beale, who had seen the report in the newspaper, and had become curious as to how the Daveys were now. They had lost contact a long time ago.

"She's in London with a Swiss family," said Caroline, delightedly. "Oh, would she come to my wedding, do you think? I would love to see her again!"

I shall tell her, she continued to herself, *that I have been tested in the fire she spoke of.*

ONE WEDDING LEADS TO...

A simple wedding was not to be, for Arthur was now in political life, and the list of guests grew. On a beautiful August day, Caroline went to the church in billowing white satin and lace, a tiara of orange blossoms about her veil, and carried a bouquet of marigold, her mother's favourite flower, and gypsophilia. Percy gave her away. It was a very merry wedding, and when she threw her bouquet, it practically fell on top of Eleanor's head.

"So much for that superstition," Eleanor said, catching it in her hands. "I will never marry!"

"You don't know what's in your future, Eleanor." Matthew Harries was by her side. "I'm selling the house and lands in Middledene and have seen a place I like in Wales. Nobody knows me there. Do you know what I am asking you?"

"I'm older than you, Matthew."

"Only by a few years. That is not of any consequence. Eleanor." He took her to one side, away from listening ears. "The last time I proposed, it was to make you respectable after the harm my brother did. Now, I ask you out of love. I do love you, Eleanor. I have your brother's blessing, in case you are concerned about that. You and I have gone astray, we understand each other. We both have indulged in excesses of alcohol, and we can keep each other straight. Do I have any chance?"

He saw the answer in her blush and her smile, suddenly as bashful as that of a maiden of seventeen.

"To be loved for myself! That is something I cannot resist, Matthew."

THE LIGHT SHINES

Arthur and Caroline had been married three years and were now in a position to visit Ireland. Caroline looked forward immensely to meeting Arthur's family. The Ellises lived in an enchanting spot near the small fishing village called Dingle. They were ecstatic to see their son, were delighted with his choice of wife, and doted on their baby son, Arthur Junior, who they snatched away every day to spoil, leaving his parents to walk alone wherever they wished.

One sunny morning, Caroline and Arthur walked along the Wine Strand at Ballyferriter hand in hand, looking out across the wild, rugged bay.

"God has been good to us," Caroline said suddenly. "Whatever happens in the future, I think I would not, I hope I would not, *lose hope*. Hope is the worst thing to lose, isn't it? When I first met you, I had no hope left. How terrible to be without hope, Arthur."

"*'The light shines in the darkness, and the darkness cannot extinguish it,'*" was Arthur's reply. He squeezed her hand.

"You brought that light to me, Arthur." She kissed him.

A soft Atlantic breeze blew into the sheltered beach and caught them in a warm embrace.

Thank you so much for reading. We hope you really enjoyed the story. Please consider leaving a positive review on Amazon if you did.

WOULD YOU LIKE FREE BOOKS EVERY WEEK FROM PUREREAD?

Click Here and sign up to receive PureRead updates so we can send them to you each and every week.

Much love, and thanks again,

Your Friends at PureRead

Printed in Great Britain
by Amazon